Praise for

ICE ISLAND

"Riveting and atmospheric. . . . In vivid, crisp prose, the story accelerates as . . . Cole and Tatum rely on their training and resourcefulness as they face hunger and below-freezing temperatures. . . . Told [in] a fast-paced third-person, this survival adventure creates an almost otherworldly experience within a treacherous and bracingly beautiful landscape. As a race for survival, this is also an exhilarating sprint through the pages."

—*Kirkus Reviews*

"The legendary Iditarod serves as both starting point and backbone for this adventure-survival tale. . . . Shahan knows her territory well and vividly describes the landscape's stark beauty and Tatum's sense of isolation. Heroic dogs, danger, and an accessible writing style add cross-gender appeal." —*School Library Journal*

"Readers attuned to the call of the wild will gobble this down like the frozen caribou strips and turkey skin treats that keep Tatum's dogs running." —*Booklist*

ICE ISLAND

sherry shahan

SCHOLASTIC INC.

ISBN 978-0-545-80221-5

12 11 10 9 8 7   17 18 19/0

Printed in the U.S.A.   40

First Scholastic printing, December 2014

for my first reader, Phillip Cole, and for Grandma Tatum—
and my youngest fans, Cooper and Chase

1

The siren blasted three times.

It didn't startle Tatum.

She'd been expecting it.

She peeked out from under her blankets. The clock read 3:46 a.m. She glanced across the tiny bedroom at her mom. Should she wake her? No. She knew what her mom would say. *You're not going out in the middle of the night, Tatum. Now go back to sleep.*

Her dad? That would be a different story. But he was on the North Slope of Prudhoe Bay inspecting pipelines for leaks. Winter was the only time the ground was hard enough to support heavy equipment. Her dad worked four on and one off—meaning he worked four weeks straight, then had a week off.

Tatum slipped out of bed and punched the stopwatch function on her Timex, a gift from her parents on her thirteenth birthday. Snow pants, boots, parka, gloves. Forty-three seconds. A musher had to be ready faster than that, she knew. Even with his fused ankle, her dad had it down to fifteen seconds.

Keep practicing, she told herself.

She tucked the blanket snugly around her pillow. It didn't look like a real person—more like an oversized teddy bear. It might fool her mom, if she didn't turn on the light.

Tatum eased out the door and crept down the back stairs. She hated sneaking around like this. But what choice did she have? The siren meant a musher was on the final stretch before town. She hoped it would be her friend Beryl.

Outside, a ribbon of light flashed over the office of the town's newspaper, the *Nome Nugget*: minus twenty degrees Fahrenheit, without the windchill factor. Tatum tightened the hood of her parka, passing souvenir shops and old-style saloons on the plank sidewalk. Her feet ached with bone-numbing cold. She stomped them to get warm. Stars dabbed the frozen sky.

The famous wooden arch stretched over Front Street: END OF IDITAROD SLED DOG RACE. Tying a mob of dogs together? Getting them to go in the same direction for a thousand miles? In the dead of winter? Everything that could go wrong usually did, and then some.

Someday I'll be out there running alongside Dad, Tatum thought. *As soon as we're settled in one place, we'll start gathering dogs for two teams.*

Her dad talked about getting rescue dogs from a shelter. "They don't have to be fast," he said. "Just strong, good-natured, healthy—and most important of all, able to laugh at my jokes."

Once, she'd told him that dog mushing felt like flying without wings. He'd smiled, hugging her. "That's how it's supposed to feel." She missed him even more at times like this.

Tatum wrapped her arms around herself, half frozen, and shuffled toward a bulky snowsuit leaning against the wooden arch. She recognized this year's champion, J.M., a young-looking giant. He'd crossed the finish line two days ago, winning in nine days, sixteen hours.

She thought it was amazing that he came out at any hour, day or night, to congratulate the teams as they finished. She knew he had to be utterly spent.

"A bit late to be out here, isn't it, missy?" J.M. asked, his fingers wrapped around a fat mug.

"I heard the siren," Tatum said. She caught a whiff of chicken soup. "I'm hoping it's Beryl."

"According to the last report, Beryl has passed through White Mountain," J.M. said. "I'm betting it's that rookie from Montana, Mack Gyldendal. He'll be one to watch in a few years."

Tatum had read about Mack. He'd turned eighteen the day before signing up for the race, and had driven by himself to Alaska in an old pickup. His dogs rode in a camperlike shell clamped onto the truck bed.

"Beryl should be close to Safety by now," J.M. put in.

Tatum sure hoped so.

Her dad had given her a guide that showed each

3

checkpoint and the number of miles in between. Safety was the last checkpoint before Nome. Just a roadhouse stuck on a sea cliff. Sometimes tired dogs used to resting at the more than two dozen checkpoints between Anchorage and Nome refused to go through Safety without stopping. They just lay down.

Tatum couldn't imagine how terrible it would be for an exhausted musher who had already gone a thousand miles to watch himself slip in the standings that close to the finish line.

Tatum kept her feet moving, trying to jump-start her internal heater, thinking about last summer. Her dad had helped her get a job at a temporary camp set up on a glacier outside Juneau. She'd spent a month there working for Beryl. Tourists were flown to the top of the glacier, where they paid big bucks for sled dog rides.

Beryl had taught Tatum the most efficient way to harness the dogs, and how to make sure their booties were snug. "Not too tight," Beryl was quick to remind her. Tatum had fed and watered the dogs too.

At night Beryl worked over a small loom, sharing stories of her life in Alaska. She sold her handmade scarves to visitors. Larger pieces, like shawls and ceremonial capes, were commissioned by a gallery in Anchorage. Still, she had to scrimp to afford the Iditarod. The entry fee alone was four thousand dollars. That didn't include the cost of flying food and supplies to checkpoints before the race.

Tatum had listened, curled up with a mug of cocoa. Sometimes, in the middle of a story, Beryl would look up and ask, "Is *haw* the command for turning right or left?" Or,

"What's a gangline?" After a while, Tatum got used to the pop quizzes.

Beryl was one tough woman. She spent winters alone in a log cabin without electricity or plumbing. "No running water," as Tatum's dad liked to say, "unless you *run* to get it."

Tatum thought Beryl's dogs were the smartest dogs in the world. Especially Bandit, the lead dog, Tatum's favorite. It takes a smart dog to understand a musher when he's shouting from the back of a sled. When business was slow, Beryl let Tatum take a team out by herself. Bandit always wagged her tail for Tatum, even when she messed up.

Beryl will be pushing hard to finish the last stretch, Tatum thought. She'd already handled everything the race had thrown at her; otherwise she wouldn't have made it this far. Lots of mushers just gave up.

Tatum turned when a checker and other race officials came out of the Sleeping Dog Café, hunched against the numbing cold. One was on a two-way radio, talking to an official out on the trail. A vet trailed behind them, looking like he hadn't slept in a month.

"Manor had to scratch," one official said. "Broke through overflow water on Norton Sound. Water soaked clean through his boots—froze solid on his feet."

"Glass slippers." J.M. shook his head. "The fool should've stopped to put on dry boots."

Tatum shivered from more than the cold.

"You know how it is," another official put in. "It's dark and forty below. You wait till the next checkpoint to sort it out."

"Then it's too late," J.M. added.

"A volunteer had to cut his boots off with an ax. Lucky he didn't lose any toes."

Tatum heard a team of dogs before they swung around the corner. "Beryl?" she asked, her hopes up.

"Nope, it's Mack," J.M. said.

She watched Mack jog in the snow next to the sled, keeping one hand on the driving bar. She tried not to show her disappointment. But she'd been hoping Beryl would finish in the top twenty—and pick up a few sponsors. A year's worth of free dog food would really help out.

Mack struggled to keep his sled going straight. The hood on his parka wasn't pulled all the way up. He swiped at icicles hanging from the hood's fur ruff.

Tatum counted eight dogs trotting in front, tails curled over backs. Two barked from inside the sled.

Most mushers started the race with sixteen dogs in harness—twice as many as they needed to cover a thousand miles. She doubted people outside Alaska thought much about it, but mushing wasn't like football or soccer. If a dog got sick or hurt and was taken out of the race, a musher couldn't substitute another player from the bench.

One of her Iditarod videos showed half a dozen dropped dogs corralled at a checkpoint. A vet took care of them until a volunteer pilot showed up. She'd laughed, watching the dogs sit patiently inside a bush plane. It was as if they flew all the time.

Mack must have dropped five or six dogs along the way, she thought. About average. Most mushers finished with between eight and twelve.

Mack shouted his bib number to an official and staggered under the famous burled arch.

J.M. slapped his shoulder, passing off the mug of soup. "Welcome to the club."

"Thanks, man," Mack said hoarsely.

Tatum congratulated him too.

"Eighteenth," an official said. "Nice job."

Mack nodded.

Tatum moved from foot to foot, watching the official jot down the time in, number of dogs in harness, and other stats. Mack scribbled his signature without taking off his gloves. Only one reporter came out for a picture.

Tatum didn't think it was right. Two days ago, when the first siren had blasted, the street had been jammed with fans and TV news crews, all cheering for J.M.

Now she watched Mack hug his dogs. "Good job, fella. How're you doing, girl?" He had a gash across his forehead, probably a run-in with a tree.

"Have you seen Beryl?" she asked.

Mack shook his head. "I've been running alone." He dug a bag from his sled and tossed out chunks of meat. The dogs inside the sled scrambled out to eat the frozen snack. Reflector tape on their harnesses winked in the dim streetlight.

"Two tired dogs is all," he told the vet.

The vet nodded, checking the dropped dogs first.

Tatum looked down the long, dark street. Her friend should have passed through Safety by now. It was only twenty miles away.

7

Only?
Yeah, right.

• • •

Back inside the small apartment, the smell of grease and cigarette smoke had worked its way up from the restaurant downstairs. It was too cold out to crack a window. Tatum quietly shrugged her outer clothes off. She nearly jumped out of her long johns when the light flicked on.

Her mom looked mad enough to spit nails. "Why didn't you wake me?"

"Sorry. But I knew you had the early shift this morning."

"It's pitch dark out there, Tatum." Then her mom looked more worried than mad. "When I said you could meet the teams coming in, I didn't mean in the middle of the night."

"Sorry," Tatum repeated quietly, and slipped into bed.

Her mom stood there awhile, like she didn't know what to say next. Finally, she turned off the light. "Beryl get in yet?"

"Huh-uh."

The ancient bedsprings squeaked loudly. "Don't worry," her mom said. "She'll come in soon."

Tatum pulled up the scratchy blanket. "Hope so."

Come on, Beryl, she pleaded silently. *Come on, Bandit.*

2

Tatum got up and rummaged around for clean socks. Morning light filtered through the thin curtains. "Mom!" she hollered, then remembered her mother would be at the café handling the breakfast crowd.

Her mom took whatever job she could get during the winter months when Dad was away. She never complained, though, no matter how seedy their accommodations.

Tatum found a pair of socks stiff with dried sweat. Good enough for another day. She got dressed quickly, wondering how many sirens she'd slept through. Beryl had probably come in hours ago.

She rushed downstairs, stepping into nature's freezer. It was easy to spot tourists here for the race. They were bundled up head to toe. Locals had a different internal thermometer. They wore light jackets and walked with their faces turned up to the sun, like it was some kind of god.

Tatum shivered, wondering if she'd ever get used to the

weather. Even in March it was so cold her breath made little dandelion puffs. She hurried along Front Street, where the Bering Sea butted up against a concrete wall.

Nome was below the Arctic Circle, but the sea closest to shore froze solid in winter. Somewhere she'd read that salt-water ice was stronger than freshwater ice. She stopped to look farther out, where ice buckled into pale blue ridges.

Tides and driving wind shattered ice as they moved it, shoving one frozen block up against another. Crack, thaw, refreeze, break. Sea ice was always on the move. Yesterday Tatum had seen two pickups out there spinning doughnuts. *Crazy!*

She made her way to the dog yard—a temporary fence set up around a parking lot—on the far side of town. On the other side of the fence, mushers were hauling buckets of food and water from a supply trailer. Most wore jeans and sneakers. Sweatshirts replaced parkas, and knit beanies were worn instead of fur. Their faces were windburned, sun-burned, scraped, bruised. Fishermen, lawyers, doctors, teach-ers, miners, artists, and natives had all taken time away from regular jobs to race.

Tatum's dad was born in Alaska and had run in the Jr. Iditarod before his family moved to Oregon. It sounded unbelievable, but he'd once fallen asleep on a training run. "Getting knocked off a sled by a sharp tree limb is an instant wake-up call!" he'd said, laughing.

Another time he'd nearly sliced off his thumb while changing a cracked sled runner. "No big deal," he'd told her. "My buddy lost his pinkie finger."

There were endless stories of mushers taking risks. In

10

1985, Libby Riddles had crossed Norton Sound during a blizzard, heading into the face of a blinding storm and cutting winds—winds that fired ice bullets.

Foot by foot, from one marker to the next, she'd left the rest of the field behind. Tatum knew that sometimes taking a chance paid off. That year Libby became the first woman to win the Iditarod. Then Susan Butcher snagged the title three years running—1986, 1987, 1988—and again in 1990. Tatum had read Riddles's *Race Across Alaska* so many times the pages were falling out.

Two days ago, Tatum and her mom had climbed onto barrels and cheered J.M. across the finish line. People crowded onto balconies, packed rooftops, and hung out windows. Snowmobiles raced up and down the narrow street. A special area was roped off for video, film and TV news crews, and wire services. Tatum had strained to see around the mob, listening for the sound of dogs.

Iditarod fever was contagious as ever.

What a drag, she thought, that the crowds dwindled after the first day.

• • •

Tatum watched an Alaska Airlines truck rumble through the entrance of the dog yard. The driver got out and started unloading kennels the size of industrial washing machines. Tatum had been doing odd jobs around town so she could buy a ticket to the Mushers Awards Banquet.

She knew J.M. would get a cash prize and a trophy, plus keys to a new pickup. The Red Lantern award went to the last musher to finish, no matter how long it took. Years ago, a guy spent more than a month on the trail. By then, the banquet was over and done with. Her bet was on Mack for Rookie of the Year.

The day after the banquet, mushers would crowd onto commercial airplanes—dogs, sled, gear, stinky clothes, and all—and fly back to Anchorage. Some mushers paid to have their dogs in the plane's cabin, where they were kept in an area separated from passengers.

Tatum laughed, remembering the story about dogs getting loose. Flight attendants chased them up and down the aisles, unable to corral them. She'd have loved to see that!

Tatum stopped at the gate. "Has Beryl Webb checked in?"

The guard lowered his two-way radio. "Couple of hours ago."

"Which part of the yard?" she asked.

He fiddled with the radio. "You got a pass?"

"Uh, I forgot it."

"No one gets in without a pass."

"I work for her." She kept at him. "And I'm late."

"Sorry," he said, but didn't sound it.

Tatum hurried around the outside of the fence, wishing Beryl had arranged clearance. She peeked through the fence slats. Inside, mushers were taking care of their teams. "Wait till next year," a stocky guy told a chocolate-colored dog that looked more Lab than husky.

Someone else was singing, "We all live in a yellow submarine. . . ."

Tatum spotted Beryl's team by a cargo container,

sprawled out in shades of black, brown, and yellow. A breeze played across their ruffs. They looked ready to run another thousand miles. One year a musher did just that—turned his team around and mushed back to Anchorage.

"Beryl!" she hollered.

"Hey!" Beryl called back. Her brick-red hair was matted into a braid. Sunglasses held a piece of cardboard over her nose. She didn't look half as good as her dogs, more like she could sleep for a week. She'd lost a bunch of weight too.

Tatum leaned into the fence. "Everything okay?"

"Nothing a hot shower won't cure." Beryl said it like a hot shower was a luxury. "Now get in here!"

"I don't have a pass," Tatum said.

"Climb the dang fence!"

Tatum found a slot wide enough for her boot. She pulled herself up, dropping down on the other side. When Bandit saw Tatum, she made a beeline for her. Bandit was black and cinnamon, except for her white muzzle and belly and a dark patch around one eye, which made her look like she was winking.

The rest of the team circled Tatum at about a hundred miles an hour, yipping happily. Tatum hugged them all, then squatted beside Bandit. "Guess you missed me!"

Bandit crawled all over her, licking her face. She wagged her tail so hard her back end shook.

Tatum wrapped her arms around the dog, kissing her on the nose. Bandit licked her whole face at once. She must've smelled last night's cheeseburger. "I've missed you too!" Tatum told her.

Tatum massaged Bandit's shoulders, which the dog

loved. Even though mushers used padded harnesses, the dogs' shoulders sometimes got sore.

"It was a long, hard haul, but they never gave up," Beryl said, cooing to her dogs constantly. "Dropped Calico and Boots early on. Upset stomachs. Bandit got us through the gorge before she tired out. Cried like a baby when I put her in the sled, even though it was only for twenty miles."

"Where did you come in?"

"Twenty-third," Beryl said. "Not bad in a field of sixty-seven."

If Beryl was okay with her finish, then so was Tatum.

Tatum helped rub ointment on the dogs' feet. Race rules said mushers had to carry enough booties to last more than a thousand miles. Even so, snow could work its way through the material and rub against the dogs' toe pads. The dogs licked her face the whole time, tails thumping the ground.

"You have the best dogs!" Tatum said.

Beryl smiled. "They're all team players."

Part of Tatum's summer job had been cleaning up after them. Just shovel their business into a wheelbarrow, right? *Wrong.* It froze to the ground hard as lead. First she had to chop it loose with an ax.

"Wish I could sweat through the pads of my feet and nose," Beryl said. "Save a fortune on deodorant."

Tatum laughed at that one.

"You know, sweat is the leading cause of—"

"—dehydration." Tatum finished the sentence. She knew it was a real danger on the trail, for both mushers and dogs.

"You're a great student," Beryl said. "It was so hot in Knik I wore my boots without socks."

Tatum knew "hot" could mean twenty degrees.

"One musher used a turkey baster to squirt water down a dog's throat," Beryl said.

"To keep it hydrated?"

Beryl nodded. "You have to be creative to be a musher."

Tatum's dad called it ingenuity.

Beryl filled an ice chest with warm water. Her sneakers crunched the snow while she bashed frozen meat into smaller chunks. "I'm heading off to teach a wilderness survival course to a group of kids in Wyoming," she said. "My flight leaves this afternoon."

Tatum dropped the meat into the ice chest to thaw. "What about the banquet? And who'll take care of your dogs?"

"I've been to a million banquets." Beryl stirred the chunks so they'd thaw faster, then scooped the doggie stew into metal bowls. "The dogs are staying here with a friend."

"What about Bandit?"

Beryl sighed, sitting back on her heels. "I haven't told her yet, but this was her last race."

"You're retiring Bandit?" Tatum couldn't believe it. "But why?"

"She'll be nine next year. Besides, she's led our team into the top twenty more than once. That's something." Beryl sounded like a proud mother. "It's time to let her younger brother take over."

Tatum buried her face in Bandit's ruff. "I'll take her," she said.

"Oh, Tatum. You know how much trouble and expense these dogs can be. Tons of exercise. And . . ." Beryl paused. "Bandit hasn't been herself lately, kinda sluggish. Maybe it's the race. But if it's something else, it could mean vet bills."

Tatum didn't hesitate. "I have a savings account." She didn't mention that it was a college fund. Or that she'd spend every cent on Bandit if she had to.

"What about your parents?" Beryl asked. "Shouldn't you run it by them first?"

"Dad'll be thrilled I'm getting a dog," Tatum said, not mentioning her mom's feelings about it.

Beryl nodded as if that sounded reasonable. She poured a twenty-five-pound sack of dry dog food into a plastic garbage bag and added Bandit's bowl, harness, and a handful of booties. "I'll mail you her vet record."

"Great."

Beryl knelt down and gave her lead dog a warm hug.

Tatum looked on quietly, knowing how hard this was for her friend.

Beryl held Bandit's ears and kissed her on the nose. Then she stood up and pulled a T-shirt from her sled. "I brought this for you."

Tatum nearly cried reading the slogan: ALASKA — WHERE MEN ARE MEN AND WOMEN WIN THE IDITAROD.

3

Tatum led Bandit down the street, towing the heavy bag over her shoulder. Her mom was going to be mad, real mad, and quick to point out her "no dogs until we're settled in one place" rule.

Worse still, the apartment they were bunking in didn't allow pets. And besides, it was too cramped for a dog. Tatum had a lot to figure out.

Bandit stayed at her heels, nuzzling her thigh. Halfway down the block her dog stopped, looking back at the dog yard. "It's okay, girl," Tatum said, feeling sad and excited at the same time. She'd never imagined she'd have a dog like this of her own.

She bent down and looked directly into Bandit's eyes. "I'll take real good care of you," she promised. "Cross my heart and hope to die."

Bandit licked her cheek.

The glare of sunlight on the frozen sea drew Tatum's gaze to a green circle a hundred yards out. Then she saw the pin and flag. Astroturf. Guys in ridiculous costumes were hitting red golf balls off the deck of a tavern. People did silly things to entertain themselves during the long winter.

Tatum stopped at the Arctic entrance to the Polar Café—a small space between two heavy doors that kept cold from seeping into the main part of the building. "Not a sound, Bandit, okay?"

Bandit cocked her head, licking the air.

Tatum hugged her neck. "Mom won't be able to resist you!"

She led Bandit through the back door into the kitchen. "Nice dog," the cook said, scratching Bandit behind her ear.

"Bandit," Tatum said, "meet Jake."

Bandit sniffed Jake's shoe.

Tatum set down the bag and peeked into the dining room, searching for her mom. Mismatched tables and chairs were tightly packed. Snowsuits and parkas hung on hooks. Boot liners littered the floor.

"Looks busy," she said.

Jake grunted, flipping two bloody slabs of meat. "As a hound in flea season."

Steaks, fried eggs, and sourdough pancakes filled plates set out under a heat lamp. Between exercise and subzero temperatures, some mushers lost more weight than was healthy. A body burned thousands of calories to keep from freezing to death.

"Who gets the steaks?" Tatum asked.

"Anyone without a plate," Jake said.

She picked up three plates, balancing one on her forearm. "Bandit, you wait here." Bandit curled up in a corner, head on front paws, watching. She seemed to know something was going on.

Tatum pushed through the swinging doors. Judging by the windburned faces and the stories, everyone in the crowded dining room was either a musher, a race official, or a vet. This was obviously a favorite mushers' hangout.

"He got sucked into a bad hole near Koyuk," one guy was saying, drawing circles on the table with his spoon. "Nearly lost his wheel dog."

"He's probably still pouring water out of his long johns," said another.

"It was so warm going through McGrath, the liver started to thaw." A guy pushed back from the table with a satisfied burp. "Turkey skins stayed solid enough."

Tatum squeezed between the tables. "Hi, Mom."

Her mom smiled, rushed over, and took the plates. "I have exciting news," she said, setting them down to grateful murmurs. "We're going to Wager."

"Ain't she a bit young to gamble?" a guy cracked.

"Not in Nevada, you fool," her mom said, shushing him. "Santa Ysabel Island."

"A hundred miles from nowhere," he said. "And colder than a tail on a brass donkey."

Tatum had heard of Santa Ysabel, an island in the Bering Sea, closer to Russia than the U.S. mainland. "Remember Maryanne?" her mom went on. "She called this morning and asked if we could fill in at her lodge while she's on vacation. Jake said he could make do without me for a week."

"She's probably going to Hawaii," the guy said with a laugh.

Tatum's mom ignored him. "She'd planned to close down, but a reservation came in from the Bureau of Indian Affairs," her mom said. "Pack your heaviest gear. Maryanne said the wind blows so hard it can be minus forty, even when the sun's out."

Tatum didn't mind moving from place to place during the winter or living out of a duffel. It was sort of like camping indoors. She took a deep breath, knowing it was now or never. "Can I bring a friend?"

Her mom stopped what she was doing and stared at her. Tatum's only friends lived near Skilak Lodge, where her parents worked April through October.

"Order up!" Jake called from the kitchen.

"Sorry, honey," her mom said, still looking surprised. "Not this time."

• • •

Nome Airport was a flurry of activity.

Tatum and her mom had tickets for the early flight to Santa Ysabel. But a soupy fog hung thick and low. Who knew when they'd be able to take off? The best estimate, late morning.

Her mom was still mad as a box of bullfrogs. "Tatum, we've been through this before," she'd whispered angrily. "We move around too much right now to have a dog. Things will be different when we have our own lodge."

She had only given in because they couldn't get ahold of

20

Beryl. "I don't know what we'll do when we get back from Wager. You know how the manager feels about pets," she'd said, then sighed. "But we'll figure something out."

Tatum had thrown her arms around her. "You're the best!"

"And Bandit needs regular exercise, even when the weather's crummy."

"No problem!"

Her mom had sighed again, long and loud. "You're so much like your dad."

Tatum didn't think that was such a bad thing.

She held Bandit's leash in a cubbyhole of a gift shop, disappointed to be missing the mushers' banquet. But Beryl wouldn't be there either.

No one fussed about a dog at the airport. There were more dogs in the forty-ninth state than people. She killed time, thumbing through a book about local history.

In the 1880s, when maps had been drawn up for this part of Alaska, the mapmaker couldn't find a reference for the point of land that stretched east of town. He'd scribbled *Name?* on a rough draft, planning to fill it in later. When the map was published, it showed Cape Nome. The name stuck.

"Do you have any books on the Iditarod?" she asked the clerk.

The woman looked up from a newspaper. "Know why the race is 1,049 miles?"

"You bet I do," Tatum said. "It's because the race is more than a thousand miles, and Alaska is the forty-ninth state."

"Most Alaskans don't know that," the clerk said, impressed.

"And it always starts the first Saturday in March," Tatum added.

"Right again."

The fog lifted around noon, leaving whispers of high clouds against a pale sky. A bush pilot came out, saying they'd be leaving in fifteen minutes. There were two other passengers on the small plane, a man and woman in Native parkas. Tatum loved the wolverine ruff and wondered if the inside fur was beaver.

Tatum's backpack was crammed with books and her Iditarod videos. Her duffel held everything else. The pilot had taken the bag of dog food. "I'll stow it with the luggage," he'd said.

She led Bandit through the small hatch door and took a seat behind the pilot, then buckled her dog in. "Bet you've flown more than most people."

Tatum tore off pieces of a bologna sandwich, letting Bandit lick her fingers between bites. She'd known having a dog would be like this. Just like this. "I love you too, girl."

Her mom sat by herself, settling in with a magazine.

"Put on your headsets, otherwise you won't be able to hear me," the pilot said. He bit into a jelly doughnut, then made a cockpit check. "These engines are noisy as skeletons on a tin roof."

"Here we go," Tatum said, hugging Bandit's neck.

They took off, flying west in a wide-open sky. Nome looked small in the endless flat landscape. As soon as they gained altitude, they leveled off, and Nome faded away. It was impossible to know where land left off and the frozen sea began.

Now Tatum understood how a hunter could wander onto a sheet of ice without knowing it and drift out to sea. Trapped, floating away from land. Nothing he could do about it, except wait for a ship or a plane to spot him—and hope one did before his frozen island melted.

The pilot switched on the intercom. "Santa Ysabel Island is about ninety miles long," he said, talking to them through the headsets. "That makes it the largest island in the Bering Sea.

"The last census put the population of Wager at six hundred and fifty three. That's fifty-nine people per square mile. My apartment building in Fairbanks has more people in it than that."

Tatum stared out the window at scattered cakes of ice floating on the water. For a girl raised in Portland, it looked like something you'd see in a movie and wonder if it was real. While her friends were watching reality-TV shows, Tatum had been glued to her dad's Iditarod videos. She knew more about dog mushing by the time she was ten than her friends would ever know about soccer or baseball.

"The native people are Siberian Yupik, and most of them speak Yupik," the pilot continued. "It's one of the two main Eskimo languages in Alaska. The word *yuk* means 'person,' and *pik* means 'real.' So *Yupik* literally means 'real people.'" He could talk to them, answer questions, and open a new box of jelly doughnuts, all without losing contact with his instruments.

"Santa Ysabel is within spitting distance of Russia," he went on like a tour guide. "The ice might look solid, but inches below the surface lies thousands of feet of stone-cold

23

water. Dozens of houses in Wager use a honey bucket for a toilet. Not a tree anywhere on the island for a poor dog to lift his leg."

Tatum glanced at Bandit, asleep and twitching. Doggy dreams.

She pressed her nose to the glass and could see the coastline of Russia and the Alaskan mainland out the same window, even though Russia was a whole other continent.

"We're within twenty miles of the International Date Line," the pilot said. "What you're looking at is tomorrow!"

Tatum laughed, wishing her dad was with them. *He'd love this!*

Her mom had called him from the airport to let him know where they'd be for the next week. Tatum got in a quick "I love you!" before they lost the connection. Telecom had constant problems with their lines on the North Slope.

A light snow began falling, and fog bubbled up from nowhere. The engine roared, working harder to cut through the heavy air. "Tighten those belts," the pilot said.

A stiff wind slammed the plane.

It dropped, lurching sideways.

Tatum closed her eyes—not praying, exactly, but wishing she was on solid ground. They hit more turbulence. The small plane vibrated. The pilot responded quickly to every jerky movement. He gripped the control wheel with both hands. Seconds passed. Minutes.

"If this doesn't clear up on our next loop," he sputtered over the intercom, "we're heading back to Nome."

Loop? We've been flying in circles?

Tatum craned her neck and studied the dashboard, a puzzle of lights, needles, and numbers.

Just then a hole broke through the marine layer. The plane roared as the nose dipped. Santa Ysabel looked small, an irregular splotch among puffy white clouds. Tatum swallowed hard, trying not to lose her breakfast, and braced herself for a white-knuckle landing.

"Flying is a hard way to make an easy living," the pilot joked, and they bounced onto the runway against a stiff crosswind.

4

An Eskimo woman met the plane, looking snug in a skin parka with feathers sewn to its sleeves and tiny beads down the front. She stepped forward, opened a piece of cloth, and held out three polished teeth. "Souvenir?"

Tatum admired the smooth brown surfaces. "Walrus?"

The woman smiled shyly. "Yes, they have been buried for many years. The rich color comes from minerals that grow inside. That is what makes them so strong."

"And rare too," Tatum's mom said. "Can you come by Fireweed Lodge later? After we've settled in?"

The woman nodded and shuffled off in her mukluks.

An off-road ATV pulled up. Tatum had never seen a four-seater before. It looked more like a topless jeep.

"I'm Dixie Dee and this is your taxi. We don't have cars here. No traffic jams. No road rage." Dixie Dee was short, with beautiful skin the color of toasted almonds. Her carved ivory earrings danced while she strapped down the duffel bags.

"Same time tomorrow?" she hollered to the pilot.

He was loading crates stamped ALASKAN KING CRABS into the plane's belly. "God willing and the sea don't rise!" he shot back.

"He doesn't just fly that plane," Dixie Dee said, settling behind the wheel. "He wears it."

Tatum and her mom squeezed in. Bandit sat on the floor, resting her head in Tatum's lap. Her mom couldn't resist petting Bandit. Tatum watched the couple from the plane walk down the road. She wondered why no one had picked them up. Maybe they lived nearby.

The ATV bounced over ruts, passing city hall, a fire station, a grocery store, and the post office. The village had a single crossroad—on one corner stood a church, on the other a rescue mission. That was about it.

Cinder-block houses were staggered in uneven rows. Snowmobiles were parked out front. Rusty engine parts littered yards. Some houses were boarded up. Dirty snow grew high on roofs.

Dixie Dee eased up on the throttle, pointing at a giant tangle of driftwood. "That's the community center—the roof is walrus skin. Don't make 'em like that anymore," she said. "Bingo, movies, dances, choir practice. And meetings, meetings, meetings."

They swerved around an oil barrel and braked in front of a double-wide trailer with a peeling sign: FIREWEED LODGE. "Door's unlocked," Dixie Dee said. "I would've filled in for

Maryanne myself, but I'm up to my britches with my own work. School's down the road."

Since moving to Alaska two years ago, Tatum's family hadn't stayed in one place long enough for her to go to school. Homeschooling made more sense. "Mom was a teacher back in Oregon," Tatum said. "So my school travels with me."

"Besides, we're only here a week," her mom added.

Dixie Dee nodded. "Maryanne's sunning herself on some beach." She let out a throaty laugh. "I came to Wager to help my sister with a new baby. That was thirty-five years ago. Drop by the community center later. I'll buy you a cup of hot cocoa."

"Thanks," her mom said. "And thanks for the lift."

Dixie Dee took off, slushy snow spraying up from the ATV's fat tires.

Tatum and her mom carried their duffels up the steps. They pushed through the door into a tiny living room. Braided rugs patched a linoleum floor. The linoleum was worn through to dark, moldy plywood in places. Shelves made from crates held books and disaster-movie videos: *The Towering Inferno*, *Titanic*, and others.

Tatum unloaded her Iditarod videos.

Bandit sniffed the baseboard, her tail wagging.

Her mom stared at Bandit as if she couldn't figure out where she'd come from. "No leg lifting in here," she said.

"Mom, she's a girl."

"That was a joke, honey."

If Mom was upset about Bandit, she'd gotten over it with the help of Bandit constantly smiling her doggy smile. Tatum's dad would love her even more.

28

Bandit's nails caught on the peeling linoleum. "She'll suffocate in here," Tatum said, adjusting the thermostat.

She unpacked the picture of her dad and set it on the TV. He looked about Tatum's age—thirteen—posing by his sled with his lead dog, Big Red. "Dad would like this place."

"I miss him too," her mom said. "Let's call him after dinner."

"Great!"

They went from one small room to the next. Extra bedding was stuffed in closets. Boxes of Cheerios and Pop-Tarts crowded the kitchen counter. An oilcloth with pictures of fishing lures covered a small table. Tatum set the garbage bag with the stuff Beryl had given her in the corner.

"Maryanne reserved two rooms for the pair from the Bureau of Indian Affairs, so we have our choice of the other six," her mom said.

Tatum shot her a questioning look.

"This is the slow time of year," her mom said. "Apparently it's packed all summer with bird-watchers from the Lower Forty-eight."

Tatum chose a room at the end of the hall. A needlepoint pillow was stitched with the saying DREAM BIG — DARE TO FAIL. The room felt cooler than the others. Better for Bandit. Tatum closed the heating vent and cracked the window. Bandit jumped onto the bed, sniffing the cool air.

Tatum set her math notebook on the dresser. Her mom had given her new problems. *Sixty-two teams started the Iditarod. Each had sixteen dogs in their team. Three teams scratched when canine flu struck their dogs. Two mushers had to scratch—one dislocated a shoulder and one just gave up. Of the teams left,*

29

each had the required eight booties per dog, either on their dogs or in the sled. Calculate the total number of booties on the trail.

Tatum knew booties could last up to ninety miles, depending on snow conditions. One book said dogs could run twelve miles an hour on a fast trail. Her dad made up questions about weather. Tatum didn't find wind speed very interesting, so she did those problems last.

"Mom?" Tatum called down the hall. She found her mother standing barefoot in the shower, scrubbing the tiles. "Is it okay if I take Bandit out?"

Her mom looked unsure. "I don't know, Tatum, it's—"

"Just to check out the store," she said, looking at her watch. "It's only three-thirty, and it won't be dark for another few hours."

"If you promise to come right back." Her mom's voice sounded like it was coming from an echo chamber. "And see if they have any fresh fruit, honey. Wallet's on my dresser."

"Will do."

Bandit plunged down the steps, trying to get a grip on the slippery wooden treads. She wound up flying through the air like she'd planned it.

"You could be in a circus," Tatum said, and hooked the leash onto the ring of her dog's collar.

Bandit followed close beside her, sniffing her way down the street as if everything belonged to her. She stopped regularly to mark the snowy ground.

Tatum smiled, thinking about her dad. He always joked, "Never eat yellow snow!"

5

Down the street, a group of boys were using bone mallets to hit rock balls. Alaskan croquet. Tatum passed other kids playing in the snow, stacking small blocks of ice like Legos. Two other kids had set a dented surfboard over a barrel like a teeter-totter. Each straddled an end, bouncing higher and higher. Where had they gotten a surfboard out here?

"Hey," she called to them.

They waved back. "Hey!"

She cut behind a house with a large plywood box in its yard, probably winter storage for meat. Several houses had walrus-skin boats in front, upside down on sawhorses. The boats' frames were similar to those she'd seen in a museum, built without nails.

Snowmobiles were parked by the store, like cars in a lot. Rifles were strapped behind seats. Icicles hung from the roof. Tatum wound Bandit's leash around a post and knelt down to hug her. "I'll be right back."

Bandit tilted her head and put two paws on Tatum's lap.

Inside, a kid in shorts and a T-shirt worked the cash register. Behind him a faded map of the Iditarod was tacked to the wall. The sweep of slopes was so massive it was hard to believe it was earth.

Someday I'll be out there mushing with Dad. We'll need two sturdy sleds and about thirty-two dogs, Tatum thought. It might take five years to gather and train two teams. By then Tatum would be eighteen, the legal age to enter the race.

An old woman in a traditional *kuspuk* pullover was talking about a renegade polar bear. "Jonah saw it on pack ice near the dump last night." She was bent over a cane, her forehead streaked with soot. "A thousand pounds of *mean*."

The kid bagged her groceries. "Better keep your dogs in tonight."

Tatum didn't want to think about what *that* meant. Her dad had taught her the Latin name for "polar bear," *Ursus maritimus*. It means "maritime bear," because polar bears hunt from sea ice. "They are the world's largest land carnivore," he'd said.

She walked past TV dinners in a freezer. Food and supplies were flown in by plane. That doubled the price. A half gallon of ice cream: nine dollars. A dusty box of laundry soap: three times as much. Who could afford these prices?

She picked up a wilted head of lettuce. *Forget it*. Bananas, apples, and oranges looked even worse. She grabbed a bag of kombu candy, her mom's favorite. She said it tasted like taffy. Tatum thought it tasted like what it was: boiled seaweed, dried and then rolled in sugar.

"Do polar bears really come into the village?" Tatum

asked the kid at the register. She'd only seen one polar bear in her life. It was a tower of stuffed fur standing upright inside a glass case in the lobby of a hotel.

The kid struck a "don't be stupid" stance. "Only when they're hungry and crabby—and they're always both. Dog is their favorite snack food," he added, making his point. "Life here isn't as romantic as it looks in movies."

Tatum paid for the candy and left.

Outside, she heard the familiar whooshing sound. A kid who looked fourteen or fifteen was being pulled by two muscled dogs. He was taller than the boy in the store, but he had the same dark eyes and straight black hair.

Riding the brake, he stopped by the door. His sled had a newer type of flip-up drag brake.

Tatum checked out his dogs. The bigger one was twice the size of the other guy. He was charcoal-gray with a black line running down his spine. His coat was long, and thick as smoke. She'd never seen a sled dog that big before. Most were in the fifty-five-pound range.

Bandit barked and pulled against her leash. The dog worked his way over, sniffing her tail. Tatum reached out to pet him. He growled, showing huge, sharp teeth. She jerked back, shaking.

The kid took off his glove and slapped the dog across his nose. "Knock it off!" he shouted.

The dog dropped his head and tucked his tail between his hind legs. Tatum felt bad, as if she was the reason he'd been punished. "Some dogs don't like to be petted," she said, keeping her voice even. "Unless they're being put in a harness."

33

"He's my uncle's dog," the boy said. "Too much wolf bred into him. He's never learned there's only one alpha male on a team—and that's the musher."

"You race?" she asked, taking Bandit's leash.

"I'm gearing up for a two-hundred-mile sprint in Kotzebue. Should have a decent snowpack for another month."

"You fly your dogs to the mainland?" she asked, surprised.

"It's easy to hitch a ride on a cargo flight," he said. "Pilots don't charge me for my dogs or equipment."

"Cool."

"Yeah."

"Is the race like the Jr. Iditarod?" Tatum asked.

"This one's fourteen and up," he said. "The winner gets a college scholarship—that's worth gold around here."

"Have you run in it before?"

"I came in second last year and got this new sled," he said easily. "Local businesses donate cold-weather gear."

"Nice."

Tatum thought about Beryl and the other Iditarod mushers, equipment packed up, switching from snow boots to rubber ones for the muddy season. Then she told him about her mom filling in at the lodge.

He nodded, like he already knew.

"I'm Tatum. And that's Bandit."

"Cole," he said. "And don't pay any attention to Wolf. He was raised in Anvil, a village on the other side of the island. Wrangell, he's my lead dog. Had him from a pup."

"Ever hear of Beryl Webb?" Tatum asked.

"Heck, yeah. She came in twelfth last year."

"Twenty-third this time," she said. "Bandit led her team through Dalzell Gorge."

Cole whistled, impressed. "That's one steep canyon—and the creek always has running water. I hear those ice bridges are pretty narrow. If your dogs slow down or cut across at the wrong place, it's Popsicle time."

"Scary stuff," Tatum said.

"Yeah, but that's not why we do it."

Tatum knew what he meant.

Cole lifted a crate from his sled, balancing it on his hip. "Too bad you can't stay until spring thaw. My grandfather and uncle spend all day walking back and forth from the village to the beach checking ice. You have to be able to read snow and ice to be a musher—only they're checking to see if it's safe to go hunting.

"They don't close school for a fifty-below blizzard," he said, setting the crate beside a snowmobile. "But when a whaling captain catches a bowhead? Everyone's a butcher, even our school librarian."

Tatum's stomach clenched. She remembered the article about whale hunting in *National Geographic* magazine. The frozen shore ran red with blood.

"Maybe I can help with the dogs?" she said. "A training run or something?"

Cole looked at her like he was trying to decide if she was serious. "How much experience do you have?"

"Some."

"*Some* won't cut it out here," he said, and took off.

6

Tatum let Bandit run loose, taking a different route back. They passed houses with drying racks that held long strips of fish frozen solid. She felt like kicking herself for not sounding more confident. *I should have told Cole all the things I did for Beryl,* she thought miserably.

Bandit barked and made a beeline for a walrus skin, sniffing the dried, curled edges. The hide was stretched flat over a section of chain-link fence and propped on fifty-gallon oil drums to keep it off the ground.

"Come on, girl."

Bandit darted behind another house where four concrete walls circled a pit the size of a minivan. Two-by-fours were nailed above them like scaffolding. An enormous, dingy yellow hide hung on the rack.

Tatum tried to look away but couldn't. The polar bear had massive paws and thick curved claws. Dark eyes stared from a powerful head. *Hunting is a way of life up here*, she kept telling herself. *But that doesn't mean I have to like it.*

• • •

Tatum tried calling her dad after an early dinner of Dinty Moore stew. She stood in the kitchen, annoyed by the constant busy signal. There was always something wrong with the darn lines! She finally gave up. *I'll try again later.*

The North Slope was one of the few places in the country with a population of less than ten people. The census didn't count workers like her dad who spent winters living out of a modular lodge.

Four months was too long for him to be gone, even with his visits. But the job paid too much to turn down. Most of what her dad earned went into the fund for the lodge he and her mom were going to build. In the meantime, they got by on their salary from working at Skilak Lodge and her mom's odd jobs.

Tatum followed her mom outside to watch the sunset. They stood on the porch, drawstrings on their hoods pulled tight. Their breath huffed out like clouds. Bandit's tail swept the porch, better than a broom.

It was impossible to tell the difference between frozen land and frozen sea. How did mushers know if they'd accidentally driven onto sea ice? Especially where the Iditarod trail hugged the shore between Unalakleet to Koyuk.

One year, a woman got separated from the other mushers in a whiteout. She'd accidentally mushed onto sea ice,

37

stopping her team a few hundred feet from open water. The winds blew the snow so hard that searchers didn't find her until the next day. By then her hands and feet were badly frostbitten.

Farther out, icebergs shimmered like giant blue rocks. "Those icebergs look like lopsided buildings," Tatum said.

Her mom nodded. "Or ghostly cruise ships."

After a short burst of light the Arctic sun vanished.

The living room felt like a furnace after being outside. Tatum hung her mittens and parka on a nail. Bandit lay sprawled by the door, where it was cooler. "Let's put on a video," Tatum said.

Her mom sat down and untied her boots. "Which Iditarod will it be this time?"

"We haven't watched 1990 lately. That was the last time Susan Butcher won. Eleven days, one hour, fifty-three minutes." Tatum slid the video in and fast-forwarded to the interview.

"If you deduct the mandatory twenty-four-hour layover—and both eight-hour layovers," her mom said knowingly. "That means Butcher covered more than a thousand miles in a little more than a week." She sat back, propping her feet on the coffee table. She laughed when Bandit sniffed her socks.

"When I was growing up we played with dolls," she said wistfully. "What ever happened to your princess pony?"

"She was pink, remember? Besides, a leg fell off in the washing machine."

"I suppose a good mother would've sewed it back on."

Tatum shrugged and punched Play. "The Iditarod is a

38

sport, as popular as football or basketball in the Lower Forty-eight, but the playing field is one million square miles," the moderator was saying.

The mushers all had haggard faces, hair poking up in greasy snarls. One guy had a black eye, swollen shut. He clutched a whole cheesecake. "Sugar and fat," he said, holding it like a hamburger. "That's what we live on out here."

"Disgusting," her mom said.

"It's not as gross as the guy who ate a cube of butter," Tatum reminded her. "Mushers feed their dogs better than they feed themselves."

One of Beryl's manuals said dogs should eat beaver or seal when it was below zero, because those animals have thick layers of fat. Fish was better when it was hot—meaning twenty degrees or warmer—because fish have lots of water in their bodies.

Tatum had asked Beryl about it. "Hot or cold, Bandit will jump hurdles for carrots," Beryl had replied.

"Thank goodness Dad gave up on this," her mom said absently.

"What do you mean?" Tatum turned sharply from the TV. "He always talks about the Last Great Race on Earth. How the two of us will be on the trail, out there together. Dad with his team, me with mine, and—"

"Oh, Tatum." Mom cut her off. "You know he can't race with that messed-up ankle of his. And it's so much worse when it's cold. Can you imagine him trying to stand on the back of a sled? For a thousand miles? In subzero temperatures?"

Tatum knew about the metal plate and screws holding

her dad's ankle together, the result of a snowmobile accident. But any time he talked about the Iditarod, he'd just laugh and say, "Heck, I'm not going to *walk* to Nome."

"All he needs is a brace," Tatum said stubbornly. "A special one with room for heat packs."

Her mom got up wearily. "Sometimes dreams change, honey."

"Not Dad's. And not mine. Not *ever*."

"That's what I'm afraid of."

Tatum switched off the video and picked up *The Call of the Wild*. It was by a famous author named Jack London. She'd bought a used paperback copy for a book report when she heard it was about sled dogs. She'd tried reading to Bandit, but Bandit just fell asleep.

Tatum was at the part of the story where Buck gets kidnapped from his family in California. He's sold to traders during the frenzied 1890s when gold prospectors swarmed to Alaska and the Yukon.

Bandit got up and went to the door.

Tatum marked her place in the book. "Again?"

She waited on the porch while Bandit piddled. Her mom came out to say good night. Tatum hugged her, even though she was still upset. Her dad wouldn't say he was going to race if he didn't mean it.

Later, in bed, she put her arms around Bandit's neck. "You're the best lead dog in the world," she said.

Bandit cocked her head, as if she understood. Tatum knew Bandit had heard the same words from Beryl a thousand times.

Bandit put a paw on Tatum's chest, licking her chin.

"Stop that!" Tatum slapped at her playfully. "It tickles!"

Bandit had to go three more times before morning. Tatum trudged down the hall in a sleepy daze. She turned on the porch light each time, watching Bandit through the window.

After the last trip Tatum slumped on her bed. She used the corner of her bedspread to wipe a thin sheet of ice off the inside of the window. That was when she saw a moving shadow. It looked like a dog team.

Cole? she wondered.

Tatum reached for her snow pants. Bandit pricked her ears and jumped off the bed. She followed Tatum down the hall and into the kitchen and watched her stir leftover stew into dry dog food. "We'd better leave Mom a note," Tatum said.

Bandit thumped the floor with her tail.

Tatum opened the front door and a blast of cold air slapped her in the face. She hunched her shoulders, trudging down the steps. It was so cold, dog drool bounced when it hit the ground. The sun peeked over a distant cliff, turning it the color of a ripe peach.

She remembered the time her dad had asked if she wanted a cup of coffee. She'd made a face. "Daddy, I hate coffee. You know that." She'd screamed when he tossed it at her. It slopped over the rim and froze in midair. She'd laughed, knowing she'd been had.

Tatum kept her eyes down, searching the snow for tracks. "Stay close, Bandit," she said, stopping to glance back. The twinkling lights were a good reference point.

On the edge of town the snow turned clean and white.

She stepped over a squat tangle of driftwood, noticing a bulky shadow in the distance. It looked like a person bent over something. But she couldn't be sure it was Cole.

Suddenly she remembered the rogue bear. Being out here was stupid. Big-time stupid. "Come on, Bandit. Let's go—"

Bandit barked.

"I guess that means *okay*."

Bandit spun in a circle, barking louder.

All at once Tatum slipped; her boot cracked through the ice. Her feet burned with cold. *What's happening?* She quickly regained her footing. Slowly, carefully, she took one small step, then another. A million needles stabbed her feet.

"Don't move!"

It was Cole's voice.

He called out something else. It was swallowed by the deafening yips of dogs. "Stand still!"

Tatum froze, trying not to panic.

In a flash Cole was beside her, helping her to his sled. The soles of her wet boots squeaked on the ice. He worked quickly to undo the laces, then peeled off her socks.

"What're you doing out here?" He glared at her. "Are you nuts?"

Tatum sank into the canvas sled bag, wiggling her lifeless toes. No, not nuts. *Stupid.* Her mind went numb as a thermal blanket appeared from nowhere.

Cole wrapped her up like a burrito, then pointed to an ice-blasted cliff. "There's a cemetery up there. Coffins and crosses under all that snow. Boats capsize. People drown." He was totally ticked off. "Kids, like my cousin . . ." He stopped and sat back on his heels. "This shore has the worst overflow on the island."

Bandit stuck her head in the sled, nudging Tatum with her nose.

"Didn't you see the driftwood?" he went on. "Everyone knows you never cross a line of driftwood. This isn't any place for a *kass'aq*."

Tatum hated that word. *Kass'aq* meant "white man," another reminder that she was an outsider.

Cole uncapped a thermos and shoved it at her. "Drink this."

She took it and sipped. It was something fishy.

He tied up his brake and lined out his dogs. "Let's go!" he called with a one-footed push.

Bandit followed.

Tatum hung on to the thermos. Her feet ached. A good sign. Pain meant she still had circulation. She tried not to think about the guy with glass slippers.

Cole was right. What had she been thinking? This wasn't the Oregon coast, where waves rolled in one after another. Sure, the sea there was wild and raged during storms, but it never stopped moving. Here, water and land froze into one giant jigsaw puzzle.

If Mom finds out what happened, she thought, *I'll be grounded into the next century.*

7

Cole stopped the sled at the lodge.

Tatum limped awkwardly up the steps, cringing at the pain in her feet. All she wanted to do was go to bed until it was time to leave this floating ice cube. The lodge was dark and quiet. Luckily her mom wasn't up yet.

The note, Tatum thought with a sudden flash. *I better rip it up.*

Back in her room, she crawled under the covers, pulling them over her head. Bandit slept at the foot of her bed, a cozy lump warming her feet. Tatum wasn't sure how long she'd been asleep when a knock startled her awake. "Hey, lazybones," her mom said, coming in. "You gonna sleep all day?"

Tatum forced herself to sit up. "What time is it?"

"Time to get up."

A blizzard had blown in while she was asleep. Ice battered the window. Stiff salt wind whipped up from the sea. It felt like the air was being sucked from the room by a giant vacuum cleaner.

Her mom settled on the bed. She had on so many clothes she looked like the Pillsbury Doughboy. "Dixie Dee called earlier," she said. "She invited us to a show at the community center tomorrow night."

Tatum didn't want to go anywhere, especially if it meant running into Cole. "You have to be smart to survive up here," her dad always said. "And more than a little bit lucky."

He always made her feel like she could do anything. Right now she felt like staying in the lodge. Putting on a movie. Letting Bandit sleep on her sore feet.

She'd been lucky.

More than a little bit lucky.

A siren blasted like an exclamation point.

"That alerts the village to danger," her mom said.

Tatum scooted up, leaning against the headboard. "Probably the bear roaming around the dump."

Her mom shook her head. "That guy isn't a problem anymore." Tatum clutched the blanket. "Oatmeal's on the stove when you're ready," her mom said, getting up. "I'm heading to the store as soon as the storm passes. You want anything?"

"No thanks." She should have said *A brain*.

Tatum stayed in bed with *Call of the Wild*. Why did dogs have to get hurt in so many stories?

It happens in real life too, she thought, sliding deeper under the covers.

She'd read about Susan Butcher's team being attacked by a female moose during the Iditarod. Two dogs were kicked to death. Tatum nearly cried every time she thought about it.

She'd asked her dad why moose were so mean. "They aren't very smart," he'd said. "And wolves are their natural enemy. If a moose sees a team of dogs, maybe he thinks it's a pack of wolves." Just because that made sense didn't mean it wasn't horrible.

Tatum reached for the leather-bound journal on the nightstand. It smelled like tobacco and burned wood. The entries charted twenty years of bone-chilling weather on Santa Ysabel Island. She wondered who had written it. Probably a friend of Maryanne's.

The Yupik language had ninety-nine words for ice, depending on its size and consistency. Tatum read the words meaning "crust on fallen snow" and "fallen snow floating on water."

Ice acts like a conveyor belt, the person had written. *It brings walrus and seals to our shores.*

Her dad kept a diary, tracking his days on the North Shore. Her mom had a notebook titled *Ridiculous Questions Asked by Tourists.* "What time do they turn on the northern lights?" "Do you take American dollars?" And Tatum's favorite, "Can you whistle for a musk ox so I can take its picture?"

Tatum had one of her own. "How far can a *kass'aq* walk on thin ice?"

Bandit wiggled under the covers. Tatum didn't stop her. She wondered what Cole had been doing out there. Maybe ice fishing. She'd seen men cut holes in ice and drop lines weighted with spark plugs. Then they'd soak strips of burlap in water and wrap up their fish. The bundles froze into rigid beams. Portable refrigerators.

Tatum dozed off and on. Then she got up and padded down the hall in wool socks and slippers. "Mom?" No answer. Flat light filled the living room; the storm had blown off. Her mom must've gone to the store.

She curled up by the window, drawing the blinds, creating her own private cave world. But she couldn't stand it. If she couldn't *be* outside, she had to *see* outside. She opened the blinds.

The next-door neighbor looked out his front door, yawned, and drifted toward the community center. A girl left a house painted a gross green color. She was pulling a sleighlike sledge toward the beach.

Bandit sat at her feet, whining for breakfast.

"You had breakfast earlier," Tatum said. "How about a snack?"

Tatum saw the petrified walrus tooth on the kitchen table. The woman who'd met their plane must have been here earlier. It really was beautiful, a shiny bronze.

Tatum went back to the window. The girl with the sledge was towing chunks of ice. *Years of living here told her where it was safe to walk*, she thought. *You can't get that kind of experience from a book.*

Suddenly her mom stormed in through the front door. She kicked it shut and tossed a bag of groceries on the couch. Cans spilled out, falling on the floor.

Bandit nosed a can of chili.

"There was an old man at the store," Tatum's mom said, shaking all over. "He was talking about a young *kass'aq* girl."

Her face was red as stewed tomatoes. She snatched a can and fired it at the bag. "I can't believe you broke your promise—"

Tatum didn't know what to say. "I—I left a note."

"Don't even go there, Tatum."

Thud.

Another dented can.

"I wasn't crazy about moving up here, you know that. But teachers all over Oregon were getting laid off . . . and your dad, he always talked about us being independent. Having our own lodge . . ." Mom swiped at her damp cheeks. "And it was in the middle of the night, Tatum. Do you have any idea? You could've died out there. What were you thinking?"

Tatum looked down, slumping lower in the cushion, drowning in the tattered cotton. Sometimes it was better not to talk—to just keep her mouth shut and take her medicine.

• • •

Tatum stayed up most of the night, sitting cross-legged on her bed. She tried to finish another chapter so she could get started on her book report. But she couldn't concentrate. She snuggled under her blankets, staring into darkness. Bandit pressed against her.

"Mom didn't deserve this," she muttered, hating herself for disappointing her mother. She suddenly couldn't remember if she had thanked Cole for saving her life.

Suck it up. That was what Dad would tell her. *Then do what it takes to make it right.*

Tatum drifted off, knowing what she would do.

The next morning her mom agreed to go to the store with her. They walked arm in arm down the icy street, not talking much. Every so often, her mom squeezed Tatum's arm, as if she wanted to make sure she was still there. Tatum squeezed back.

She used part of her allowance to buy the ingredients. Back in Portland she had had a chart listing chores. Now she pitched in whenever she could; there was always something that needed doing.

Later, at the lodge, she mixed raw hamburger in a bowl with powdered eggs, brewer's yeast, dry dog food, and honey. She shaped a dozen fist-sized balls. *Honeyballs.* Dogs loved them. Bandit got the first one and whined for more. But Tatum wrapped up the rest.

Her mom was in the living room, reading. "I packed a treat for Cole's dogs," Tatum said. "A thank-you for . . . you know, yesterday morning."

Her mom looked up from her book and nodded. "I'll get my parka," she said, marking her place with a postcard. "Cole lives with his grandfather. It's the house with the polar bear hides."

Tatum's stomach knotted. She told herself hunting was like fishing, only with a rifle. It was necessary to survive here.

They were heading out when Dixie Dee pulled up. A guy with a small suitcase climbed down from the ATV. He was short with a shiny round face and spiky black hair.

"He needs a room," Dixie Dee said, before speeding off.

"Thirty minutes and I'm coming after you," her mom said.

Tatum promised. "Twenty minutes max."

Her mom sighed and looked straight at Bandit. "Don't let that daughter of mine get into any more mischief."

Bandit barked, smiling her doggy smile.

Tatum hurried off, her pack loaded with honeyballs. She wondered what the guy was doing here. The small thermometer clipped to her parka read five degrees. Bandit dashed ahead, happy to be outside.

Few people in Alaska knocked when visiting. Tatum did, though, not used to the custom. An old man answered the door. Cole's grandfather. He and Cole had the same nose and almond-shaped eyes. The man wore baggy jeans with suspenders. His baseball cap said RUST HAPPENS.

"Welcome! Welcome!" He ushered her into a room so cluttered there was barely space to turn around. The windows were coated with smoke from the wood-burning stove. Bows, old and new, hung on nails by bearskin pants and sealskin mukluks. It was too warm, stuffy. "And bring your dog!"

Bandit pushed in, trotting over to a cat. They sniffed each other, tails waving.

"Sit! Sit!" The man's wrinkles danced in the smoky yellow light. "Warm yourself!"

Tatum shrugged out of her backpack. "Is Cole home from school?" she said.

"He went to the airport to sell crabs to a group of photographers flying in for the day," he said with a bunched-up smile. "Visitors are always disappointed to learn we no longer live in *nenglus*."

"I beg your pardon?"

"Dugouts made of ice and snow. You call them igloos," he said. "They even ask to see penguins!"

Tatum laughed; she'd heard the same thing. Penguins didn't even live in the Northern Hemisphere. "I brought something for Cole's dogs," she said, opening her pack.

Cole's grandfather eased her into a chair that looked like it had been upholstered a hundred years ago. He put on a pair of reading glasses and set a scrapbook in her lap. He smiled at her over the glasses' rims, tapping old photos of men in seal-gut parkas. Faded images of hunters standing beside walrus-skin boats, harpoons in hand.

"That is me," he said. "Before the noisy voices on TV and loud engines of snowmobiles."

He brushed newspapers off a table and picked up a walrus tusk. "One day this will be a miniature sled. The traditional kind with graceful rails and a sturdy basket. Or maybe a drum handle?"

Tatum loved old-style drums and their handles carved from fossilized whale bone. "Are you a carver?"

He nodded, smiling. "This would also make a fine doll, in fur clothing with beaded trim. The more energy that goes into a carving, the greater its power," he said, turning the tusk over in his hand. "I have many totems in a museum called Smith-somebody. Have you heard of it? It is in the capital of Washington, DC."

"The Smithsonian," she said. "I've been there."

"Then maybe you know why certain things are more

valuable inside a glass case than they are alive and being used? I do not understand how a totem can protect a hunter if he does not wear it." He made what sounded like a short speech in Yupik, grunted, and then switched back to English. "We must live in two worlds today."

Cole came in and stopped, looking surprised to see Tatum. "Guess you can walk on those feet," he said, closing the door with a bang.

Tatum felt her face burn. "I brought a treat for your dogs."

Cole brushed by her, stuffing a wad of bills into a jar on the TV. "That should cover this month's electric bill," he said. Then, without another word, he turned abruptly and disappeared down the hall.

"Heating oil! Propane!" his grandfather barked. "I did not even know what money was until I was ten years old!"

Tatum told Cole's grandfather good-bye, then called to Bandit, who was still sniffing the cat. She left the bag of honeyballs on the cluttered table.

8

Tatum moped around the lodge the rest of the day, helping out. She rolled up rugs, swept floors, hung laundry outside. After it froze, she shook out the ice. That was how locals dried wet clothes this time of year.

She felt bad for the guy who'd flown in earlier. He'd planned to surprise Maryanne. He looked sadder than a sick puppy to find out she was on vacation. He didn't waste any time booking a seat on the next day's flight out.

Tatum's mom went on a bread-baking binge, humming while she measured and kneaded. "There's a small sled in the storage shed," she said, patting the dough into a fat ball. "It's perfect for a one-dog team."

Tatum shrugged. "Maybe."

Her mom draped a cloth over the bowl and held Tatum by her shoulders. "You're too young to give up on your dreams," she said, staring into her eyes. "We . . . Your dad and I . . ." She paused, thinking. "We just want you to use the brains you were born with."

"I know, Mom. I messed up. Big-time."

"Everyone messes up, honey," her mom said. "It's part of life."

Tatum listened.

"The point is to recognize mistakes for what they are— and learn from them."

Tatum nodded. "I'll try."

While the dough rose, they pulled cans from the shelves. Tatum dusted them off, checking expiration dates. She stared at the date on a can of peaches. It was the same month as her birthday. She'd be fourteen in August.

Mom's right. I'm too old to keep making stupid mistakes. She chucked an ancient can of sauerkraut.

They finished cleaning out the cupboards, then started in on the freezer. "Thought I'd wear my bone earrings tonight," her mom said, smiling. "You know, sort of dress up."

• • •

Tatum put on her mukluks with the musk ox trim, a present from her dad's last trip to the North Shore. She decided to leave Bandit at home. "Sorry, girl," she whispered before leaving. Outside she turned and saw Bandit watching them from the front window, nose pressed to glass.

Halfway down the road, Tatum wiped snowflakes from her face, feeling strangely warm. An ATV sped by, pulling a toboggan crammed with kids. They giggled with fur-wreathed faces.

A bear guarded the front door of the community center. It looked large as life, only carved from a block of ice. A group of huskies huddled near an old-fashioned sled. They were old, with cloudy eyes and ragged ears.

The biggest one licked a sore paw. He didn't make any sound at all, like it was too much trouble to breathe. He'd probably had a hard life—like the dogs in the book Tatum was reading. She knelt in the snow to pet him. He looked grateful for the attention.

"We welcome you!" An elder stepped out of the shadows. He wore fur pants and an antler hat.

"*Quyana.*" Her mom tried the Native word for "thank you." It sounded like she was sucking on a Popsicle.

His face lit up. "Excellent!"

He ushered them inside and hung up their parkas. There wasn't really a stage, just a space in the middle of the room ringed by chairs. Punch bowls and dessert platters sat on pool tables. It seemed like half the village was there.

Dixie Dee wound through the crowd, waving at them. "You made it!"

Tatum waved back.

"I've been stranded in blizzards and wounded by harpoons," Dixie Dee said, mostly to Tatum. Then she rolled up her sleeve, showing an ugly scar. "That was one bucking chain saw. We all have our stories. Now you have one too!"

Tatum's mom sighed. "Let's hope it's her first *and* last one."

"That would mean the end of life!" Dixie Dee said.

Her mom didn't look convinced.

Dixie Dee led them to a pair of folding chairs. She

introduced her family. "This is my sister Chiklak—Chickie for short. And her husband, Tomagunuk—Tommy."

"Eat!" Chickie held out a plate with strips of smoked salmon. "You're too skinny!"

"Thanks," Tatum said, taking a piece. She chewed the tough fish, listening to the musical jumble of Yupik syllables. One niece had a round belly and was knitting a small sweater, pulling each stitch tight to keep out the cold. Another of Dee's sisters filed bone jewelry.

They jabbered in a weird mix of Yupik and English. Dixie Dee would catch herself. "This winter the ice is too thin," she said, translating. "There's an old Eskimo proverb, 'If you're going to walk on thin ice, you might as well dance.'"

Tatum's mom actually smiled.

Tatum was happy to see her relax a little.

The lights dimmed and the hall grew still. Cole's grandfather came out in a long hooded outercoat—fur and beads decorated the front—and moved into the spotlight.

"He's the keeper of our knowledge, just like a library," Dixie Dee said in a hush. "Everyone calls him Grandfather."

"*Quyanaghhalek tagilusi,*" he said in a powerful voice. "Welcome. Thank you for coming."

He talked about traditions and values and the type of behavior he expected in the village. "When I was growing up snow fell by the end of August. By September we knew it was time to send our children back to school. Now it is different . . . some years it does not snow until December."

The room was quiet as a church.

"Ice is a barrier, but it also protects us from deadly swells. Today, severe storms come in quickly and without warning."

He slipped into Yupik, his voice calm, but when he spoke English, he sounded agitated. "Soon we will rope ourselves together and walk out onto the frozen sea to chop breathing holes for seals. Maybe they will come. Maybe not."

Soft murmurs rose.

"Last season our village struck the quota of bowheads allowed by the IWC."

Dixie Dee whispered, "The International Whaling Commission limits the number we can hunt."

"Even though the number of bowheads is increasing," Chickie added.

Grandfather shook his head sadly. "Only half of the whales struck were landed on shore. I blame TV and video games for killing our ancient ways."

Murmurs peaked, then fell.

"In our language the same word means *listen* and *obey*. When we listen to the elders, we obey them." His voice changed when he looked around the room. "We must teach our children the traditions. Only then will they be ready to face whatever the outside world brings."

Dixie Dee leaned over. "Young people listen out of respect, but most of them don't believe the old ways will lead to a happy life."

Tatum wondered what Cole believed.

"The Bering Sea is our garden. . . ." Then Grandfather shouted something in Yupik and called to a group of boys in fur capes with black-tipped feathers. They stepped forward, holding up wooden masks with toothy grins.

Even with the mask, Tatum spotted Cole. He stood taller than the others, and was one of the few boys not fidgeting with his cape. He looked like he belonged up there, proud in his Native costume.

Girls in fur headdresses came out next, taking their places.

Elders stood together, each holding a flat drum with a painted design. The drum handles were carved from tusks. Slowly, they began beating them with their palms. Their eyes stared straight ahead, as if looking back in time.

"The drum skin comes from the stomach of a whale," Dixie Dee whispered. "Sometimes from the bladder."

At least they use every part of the animals they hunt, Tatum thought.

She and her mom had gone on a special outing to see an exhibit at a museum in Anchorage. Displays showed bones used in housing material and how vertebrae were fashioned into furniture. Baleen, a type of built-in strainer that whales use to filter food, made good insulation for boots. Nothing was wasted.

Dixie Dee explained that the boys shuffling their feet and swinging their heads from side to side were dancing stories of life on the island: paddling boats and hurling harpoons. They landed imaginary whales and butchered them in a way that was more than storytelling. Kids from the audience ran up to help. The girls bent over, gathering invisible berries, a beautiful dance that turned into a song.

The drumbeats grew louder and the dancers twirled with strange movements. They pushed toward the floor with their hands, palms down, then pushed toward the ceiling, palms up.

"Dance of the basketball," Chickie said, and laughed. "We have dances and songs for everything!"

When the performance was over, people clapped and moved into the circle. A woman began singing; others swayed and danced. Soon the whole room was alive with music and laughter.

Tatum stood up, feeling warm in a new way. Her mom was right. She couldn't give up her dreams.

Cole's grandfather walked toward them, carrying a large ceramic pot. Cole was behind him, holding bowls and spoons.

"Eskimo ice cream," Grandfather said. "It is traditional."

"Thank you, Grandfather," Tatum said, and took a bowl and spoon.

He nodded, smiling.

Tatum knew it wasn't the same as the Eskimo Pies she used to eat in Portland. This type had shredded salmon and berries whipped in seal oil. She took a polite bite and tried not to make a face.

"The dogs liked the honeyballs," Cole said, almost sounding friendly. "Wolf inhaled his."

"Beryl showed me how to make them," she said. "Last summer on Mendenhall Glacier." Then she told him all the things she had done up there, including taking the dogs out on her own.

Cole didn't say anything. But he no longer looked at her like a know-nothing *kass'aq* from the Lower Forty-eight.

9

Bandit whined, pacing by the door.

Tatum threw off her covers. "Again?"

She didn't bother getting dressed, just shuffled in her long underwear down the hall. She opened the door and stared into the dark morning. Darkness stared back. She flipped on the porch light. It gave the snow an eerie glow. "Don't go far, okay?" Sometimes she sounded exactly like her mom.

Bandit trotted down the steps.

A few minutes later, Tatum let her back in. "You could live outside, huh, girl?" She brushed snow off Bandit's back. "That's what you do during the Iditarod. Live in the wilderness twenty-four-seven."

Her mom was in the kitchen on the phone to Wager Airport. With her free hand, she poured buckwheat batter onto a hot griddle. The circles bubbled up and she flipped them.

"I confirmed our flight to Nome—we leave in three days," she said, hanging up. "The weather's supposed to hold, if you can trust the Weather Channel."

"If you don't like the weather, wait five minutes," they blurted at the same time, and laughed. People in Alaska said it all the time. It was a good description of the ever-changing conditions up here.

"Didn't people from the Bureau of Indian Affairs have reservations?" Tatum said.

"They should've arrived yesterday." Her mom set a steaming platter of pancakes on the table. "Maybe they'll come in today."

Tatum uncapped a jar of chokeberry syrup. Chokeberries. Bearberries. Salmonberries. Alaska had fifty different types of wild berries. "When's spring going to get here?"

"The last month Dad's away is always the hardest," her mom said, sliding into a chair. Bandit sat beside her. She didn't beg, just rested her head on Mom's slippers. "We'll be back at Skilak Lodge before you know it."

Tatum couldn't wait. She missed her friends too.

They finished eating without saying much else. By then the sun had hauled itself up from the other side of the world. It looked like a picture-postcard day. Tatum helped clean the kitchen, then got dressed.

Her mom looked up from her coffee when Tatum opened the back door. "Be careful, okay?"

"I will."

"And don't forget to drink plenty of water."

Tatum nodded. It was easy to forget her water bottle when it was so cold outside fish could ice-skate.

The storage shed looked like it had been spun on its side. She climbed over a canoe and tubs of seal oil for lamps. An outboard motor was patched with electrical tape. Fishing nets and floats were tangled with rotting traps. Most were made from branches and roots. Bandit sniffed everything.

Tatum saw the sled her mom had mentioned. She was surprised it had plastic runners. In the early days, mushers made sleds from hardwood, strapping strips together with rawhide. She'd only seen ivory runners in a museum. They were strongest of all.

She dragged the sled outside, scrubbing away years of grime and spiderwebs. She studied it, amazed. It was the same kind of sled her dad had had as a kid. "A lucky sled," she muttered to herself.

Bandit jumped up, balancing on her hind legs. She pawed the air with her front feet. "You look like a wild stallion," Tatum said, grinning. "Come on. Let's make an obstacle course."

Bandit landed on all fours and trotted in a happy circle.

Empty oil drums seemed logical, though she quickly discovered they were heavier than they looked. She just about busted a gut trying to roll them into place. She stood back, out of breath, and surveyed her work. Not bad for a simple course.

Bandit barked—ears pricked, eyes wide, ready to go.

Tatum decided the sled needed weight. She went back to the shed for logs and a couple of old tackle boxes.

"Bandit, you're lead dog, wheel dog, swing dog, and every other dog. You're my one-dog team." She stepped tentatively on the runners and gripped the handlebar. "Okay, girl. Let's go!"

Bandit strained against her nylon harness, taking off with a jerk. The runners barely touched the ground. Bandit acted like this was a race—a race she'd run many times.

If Tatum remembered half of what Beryl and her dad had taught her—or half of what she'd read and seen on videos—maybe, just maybe she wouldn't wind up on her bottom. She leaned to miss the first drum, pretending it was a ditch. The next one was a boulder, followed by a series of sled-busting turns.

The sled is alive, she thought. *It breathes when it moves.*

"Gee!" she called, hoping that was the command to turn right. She was relieved when Bandit made a wide right turn. Now she remembered that *haw* meant go left.

They rounded another corner and the sled sent snow flying. Tatum held on, smiling from the inside out. She'd never had so much fun. She tried standing with all of her weight on one runner, lost her balance, and stumbled off. She jogged awkwardly, grasping for the bar. Wet snow soaked her pants.

Bandit glanced over her shoulder. *What are you waiting for?*

Scrambling onto a moving sled wasn't easy. "Whoa!" Bandit slowed until Tatum got back on.

The loop on Mendenhall Glacier had been dragged smooth with a bridge timber. It had wide, easy turns. The ground here had melted and refrozen in hard clumps. It was about as smooth as a washboard.

Don't be so stiff! she scolded herself. *Use your knees like shock absorbers.*

"Haw!"

Bandit cut left, missing a drum.

"Atta girl!"

Bandit picked up her pace. The sled bounced over the jagged ground and slammed against a hole. Bandit swung in a tight turn, and the sled tipped on its side, going into a long slide. Fishing lures flew everywhere.

Tatum staggered and fell hard. She rolled to her knees, watching the sled fly over a slick spot. "Bandit!"

She heard the ATV before she saw it.

Dixie Dee corralled Bandit on an abandoned porch and untangled the lines. Then she hooked the sled to her bumper. "I'll tow it to the lodge," she hollered back.

Tatum sat freezing in the snow.

So embarrassing!

• • •

The next day she fell when the sled skidded on glare ice, then again when Bandit chased a seagull. "At least there aren't any trees to run into," she mumbled, refusing to give up.

She thought about the history of the Iditarod. In 1925 it had seemed as if a battering snowstorm would blow the Alaskan territory off the planet. Yet word had moved like greased lightning: Eskimo kids in Nome had come in contact with the highly contagious disease diphtheria, also called black death.

The hospital in Anchorage had the only serum in the territory. How could it be transported to icebound Nome in the shortest possible time? Flying a bush plane in winter was too dangerous. They came up with another plan.

Tatum tried to imagine the brave mushers and their teams of muscled dogs carrying the serum 647 miles in a relay. It had taken five and a half days. The blizzard refused to let up, pushing the windchill factor to a hundred degrees below zero. The serum arrived frozen but still usable. Thankfully, every kid had been saved.

Tatum quivered in her boots. *Sometimes real-life adventures are more unbelievable than stories in books!*

After lunch something shifted, her speed or her rhythm. The whooshing sound began to feel like her own breathing. She felt like she was flying. Bandit was her copilot.

On their way back to the lodge Tatum saw Grandfather working on the hull of an old-style *angyapik* boat. He was using an ulu knife to scrape off barnacles. The keel was ivory—around here that meant walrus tusk. It was long and sleek, stable for the choppy Arctic Sea.

Tatum pictured him shoving off in search of bowhead whales, in a gray haze of sea fog.

"Haw!" Bandit turned right.

"Hello, Grandfather. Is Cole around?" Tatum asked, stopping by the upside-down boat.

"Soon the ice will break up," Grandfather said, staring at the frozen sea where wind whipped up snow tornadoes. "The shiny black heads of seals will appear from nowhere. This year the whales will come early—I feel it. One bowhead feeds the whole village. We celebrate with games and dances, and eat and eat."

"Is Cole still at school?" She tried again.

"When he was young he followed me everywhere—learning everything I could teach him. He could not wait until he was old enough to go whale hunting. One spring a boat capsized and people drowned. Now his mother forbids him to go out with us."

Tatum didn't know what to say to this. She watched Grandfather stretch a tanned skin over the hull.

"I soak the walrus skin in salt water," he said. "That is the best way to loosen the hair from the hide. Only then do I stitch the skins together."

She didn't ask if he wanted help. Repairing a boat was man's work.

"Life outside is changing our world. We are losing our culture, losing our roots. How can a living thing grow if its roots are cut? Half of our village is on welfare, and few of us can afford the high-priced food in the store. Many of our men drink too much."

Tatum knew he didn't expect an answer.

"Cole is the only young person in our village who uses a *qamiiyek*—I mean, a *sled* to go to school. He knows ATVs scare the seals.

"He will never leave the island, not like the others with their dreams of fast cars and fancy houses. The spirits live inside him. They live inside you too, little *kass'aq*." He looked up, his dark eyes shining. "Remember that and you will always be safe."

He nodded with a gentle smile. It was the kind of smile that reaches out. "We are all part of the land," he said softly.

• • •

Later in the afternoon, Tatum gave Bandit a good brushing, then settled on the couch with her notebook. Her mom had given her a choice of three essays: *Global warming—fact or fiction? What would the earth look like if we didn't recycle? Is sled-dog racing cruel to animals?*

Tatum chose the last one. She could write a book about how well mushers treated their dogs. Dog food was flown to checkpoints before the race. Bales of straw were dropped for bedding. Key spots had vets in case dogs needed special attention. These dogs loved to pull. They lived to run.

She smiled at Bandit. "Want to go out again tomorrow?" Bandit licked the air excitedly.

Tatum had just finished writing an outline for her essay when the front door flew open. Cole came in, bareheaded. Not even a parka. Just an old sweatshirt splattered with paint. He set a squat jar on the coffee table. "Pickled gull eggs. They're sour, like dill pickles."

She studied the water in the jar. It was a weird green. "Thanks."

His eyes landed on the picture on the TV.

Tatum closed her notebook. "That's my dad as a kid. He grew up in Homer."

Cole dropped into a chair, looking at home in the lodge. "He had sled dogs?"

"Yeah, he ran the Jr. Iditarod a couple of times. Then his

family moved to Oregon," she said. "He brought us back here a little over two years ago. He's working in Prudhoe Bay for the winter."

"Drilling?"

She nodded. "And construction."

"My father was on the first pipeline crew," Cole said. "Now he and my mother work in a fish-canning plant in Ketchikan. At night Mom makes booties for my dogs. She says each stitch brings us closer together."

He picked paint off his fingers, talking about his brothers and sisters. "They left the island after high school to find work. They promised to come back, and who knows, Johnny might. He loves it here ... loves to hunt. A good hunter can still make a decent living.

"Next time I'll bring pickled moose stomach," he said, getting up and stretching. "It's sweeter."

Tatum made a face.

"Gotcha!" He paused at the door, as if he'd forgotten something. "I saw you out there with your dog. My team could use some competition before Kotzebue." He shrugged. "Just a short run—twenty or thirty miles. No one around here is interested."

Tatum forced herself to breathe. Was he serious?

"Thought I'd go out in the morning before school," he said, opening the door. "If you're up for it?"

Tatum and her mom were flying back to Nome the day after tomorrow. It was now or never.

10

Tatum blabbed through a dinner of chunky potato soup. "Cole's training for a race in Kotzebue, a hundred-mile sprint," she said. "There's a roadhouse at the halfway point, where they have a ten-hour layover. But there isn't a road to get there, so race officials have to be flown in. A ham radio operator too."

"He's flying his dogs to the mainland?" Her mom mopped her bowl with a chunk of homemade bread. "That must cost a ton of kibble."

"Pilots don't charge him."

Tatum didn't stop talking about the race until the dishes were washed and dried. "Mom?"

Her mom turned, raising an eyebrow. "Sorry, honey, the answer is no."

Tatum felt the blood drain from her veins. "But you can't say no until I ask the question."

Sometimes her mom measured her words, one teaspoon

at a time. Now she bit her lip, frowning. "Does it have to do with dogs?"

"Just a training run," Tatum said, ready for an argument. "It'll push his team to go faster. We'll be side by side the whole time."

Mom's frown deepened.

Tatum sucked in enough air to fill a wind sock. "We won't even leave the village—just race back and forth on the main drag."

A lie.

A small one.

It nagged at her like a pebble in her sock.

Her mom slouched at the kitchen table. She picked up a towel, twisting it. "Let's try to get through to Dad," she finally said. "And see what he says."

• • •

They never got through to the North Slope. But Mom gave in. "We both know what Dad would say." She said that while rubbing Bandit's head so hard Tatum thought her dog would get a bald spot. This was really hard for her.

Tatum found Cole's phone number in Maryanne's address book. He told her to pack like it was a real race. "Extra socks, and a headlamp, if you have one," he said. "And a big plastic mug."

Tatum unloaded her duffel, spreading everything on the bed: heat packets, matches, two pairs of wool socks, a fleece-lined face mask, goggles, a hair scrunchie, and extra batteries for her headlamp. She talked to Bandit the whole time, although she was really talking to herself, afraid she'd forget something.

Trail mix made a high-powered snack: nuts for protein, M&M's for energy, and pretzels just because. She wrapped a loaf of French bread in heavy foil, then found a small package of carrots in the freezer.

Most everything fit in her backpack. Dog food and Bandit's bowl went inside a garbage bag. It would all go in her sled. Except Bandit's carrots; they'd be in her pocket.

Tatum set the alarm on her watch for 6:15 a.m. When it went off, she dressed quickly, not bothering to time it, and fixed a breakfast burrito. Bandit nosed food around her bowl until it was almost gone.

"Excited, girl?"

Mom staggered into the living room, yawning in a flannel robe and bunny slippers with floppy ears. "Better bootie up before going out," she said, half-asleep.

Tatum tossed four booties to her. "Thanks, Mom."

Her mom squatted down and scratched behind Bandit's ears. Bandit gave her face a sloppy lick-bath. "I forget, does the strap go in front or back?"

"In back. But not too tight."

Tatum decided to put the harness on inside too.

"And honey?"

Tatum kissed her mom on the cheek. "I love you too."

Her mom leaned against the doorjamb, watching them head into the cold, dark morning. "Don't make me regret this!" she called after them.

"I won't! I promise!"

"Take care of each other!"

"We will!"

• • •

A floodlight lit Cole's yard, turning the snow a runny egg-yolk color. "Hey!" she hollered. He was fastening a ski pole to the side of his sled with duct tape. Ski poles made trusty walking sticks. Tatum figured he'd packed a camp stove, sleeping bag, snowshoes, and other gear to make sure the sled had the same weight as it would during a race.

"Most of these guys are my uncle's dogs," Cole said. "He names them after Alaskan mountains. I'm taking seven dogs to Kotzebue."

"That's all?"

"Three more are waiting for me there—a friend's dogs. I worked with them last summer. They pulled a cart with wheels," he said. "The rules say no fewer than seven dogs and no more than ten."

"So they've all raced before?"

"All but Wolf. And he thinks he's boss because he's the biggest. But I raised Wrangell and Alyeska. They're both smarter. I usually hitch up the cat, but her harness broke."

Tatum laughed and glanced from dog to dog. She wondered if any of their ancestors had been in the original serum run.

One of her history lessons had covered the Klondike Gold Rush, which had begun in the late 1890s. In those days, dog teams hauled ore, mail, supplies, and people. Later, airplanes took over the mail routes, and gold fever cooled down.

She petted the mishmash of huskies. They weren't any different from the dogs she'd seen in the Iditarod. She wished her gloves had fur so she could turn them inside out. The thermometer on her parka read twenty below zero.

Ursus maritimus *could freeze out here*, she thought, feeling bad that the rogue bear had to be shot.

Cole hitched four dogs to each sled. Wrangell took the lead on his team. Brooks chewed the tugline that connected Alyeska's harness to the gangline, and Denali chewed on Alyeska's ear. Wolf took position as swing dog.

Bandit was leader on Tatum's team. Wolf acted like he didn't want her there. His head was down, his jaw jutting out, all snarls and teeth. If he hadn't been hooked to Cole's line, he would have taken a bite out of Bandit's rear end.

Bandit ignored him, tossing her head around. *Let's go!*

"We'll switch 'em up later," Cole said.

"Sounds good."

"Most people think speed wins races. But endurance, that's what counts." He tied up his brake and stepped on the runners. "Pacing isn't everything—it's the *only* thing."

Tatum knew that.

She checked her watch, grateful for the lighted numbers: 6:50 a.m. This time tomorrow she'd be packing for Nome.

And suddenly, they were off.

Bandit sprang forward with such force Tatum had to grapple for the handlebars. A lucky grab; she didn't tumble off.

The dogs trotted down the main road, yipping with excitement. Leaving the village, the road narrowed to an old game trail that roped its way around a cliff. Tatum hated breaking her promise to her mom. *We won't be gone long*, she told herself. Cole had to be back for school.

The dogs jogged by a field of ice-covered boulders, then climbed steadily toward a saddle. Tatum found a rhythm, keeping her eyes on the dogs. "Easy now," she said above the quiet *shush* of the runners. "Easy there."

Cole looked back, the light from his headlamp bobbing. He shouted something, then disappeared around a curve. Tatum followed as closely as she could.

Minutes slipped into an hour. The sky grew pale, but the sun wasn't really up. When you're on the edge of nowhere it takes forever for the sun to fully rise. First it has to wake up all of North America.

An hour later, it had turned the top layer of snow to slush. Cole's team looked like they were swimming down the trail. Snow sprayed up from his sled like the wake behind a speedboat. Tatum hit a series of ruts, *bam-bam-bam*. She held on tighter, keeping her legs flexible.

Soon Cole was a dot the size of a blackbird. How had she gotten so far behind? He made a half circle, dragging his boot in the snow. "You okay?" he asked when she caught up.

Bandit slowed beside his sled, sniffing Wrangell. Alyeska yipped, getting in on the act. Cole tossed turkey skins to both teams. The dogs swallowed the half-frozen snack, barely chewing. Bandit rolled around, begging for a scratch. Tatum rubbed her absently, taking in the broad expanse below. Distant brown clumps looked weird in all that white.

"Caribou," Cole said, digging out binoculars. "Brought here in the nineteen hundreds after a famine nearly wiped out everyone on the island. Those who didn't starve boarded a ship for Nome.

"Check out those feet. Built-in snowshoes." He handed her the glasses. "Fat reserves get them through the long winter."

Tatum focused on the cinnamon-brown bodies, their long white necks and snowy manes. The herd stood motionless, antlers gleaming, as if posing for a picture.

"It's the law of the wilderness," Cole said. "If you shoot a big animal, you have to gut it while the carcass is still warm and share the meat with the rest of the village."

Tatum refused to think about killing one of these magnificent animals. "They look at home out here in their heavy winter coats."

Cole swapped the position of the dogs on both teams. Not easy since they were too excited to hold still. Bandit barked from the wheel dog position, directly in front of the sled. Instead of leading, she'd help steer.

"Bandit looks like a puppy compared to Denali," Tatum said, sizing up the wheel dog on Cole's team.

Cole repacked, ready to go. "She can handle it."

Tatum went to the front of her team and walked Alyeska in a U-turn, until he faced the village.

Cole hesitated. "We aren't going back yet."

"What about school?"

"Kotzebue's only ten days away—this is the first time all winter I've gotten to train with another team," he said, back on his runners. "Thought I'd play hooky."

Tatum swallowed, trying to calm her nerves. "But my mom," she said with an uneasy feeling. "I told her . . ."

He tried to shrug, which was impossible in his heavy parka. "Go back if you want to."

She wanted to tell *him* where to go. But she knew better. "I thought we'd *race* back," she said stubbornly.

"No way I'm letting this weather go to waste," he said, being just as obstinate. "Tie up the dogs behind the house when you get there."

His gaze went from her to his dogs and back. At first she thought he might change his mind. He had to know it wasn't safe to split up. Then he gestured at a distant peak, washed in pale light from last night's moon.

"The trail winds around down there," he said, taking off. "Stay close to me. It's a nasty hill."

11

Snow began falling, lightly at first.

"Easy now," Tatum called to her team. They slowed going down the steep hill. She strained to see Cole's orange parka, searching for his tracks. The ache in her gut told her she should have gone back. She could spend the rest of the day sledding in front of the lodge. If Bandit got bored, she'd set up another obstacle course.

Her fingers started throbbing, a dull pain that shot up her arms. She'd been strangling the handlebars. Snow was falling harder now. She pulled up her neck gaiter, slid her goggles in place.

Stupid Weather Channel never got it right!

What would her dad tell her to do? His voice flooded her head. *Trust your gut, Tatum. You know more than you think you do. Just be smart—play it safe.*

She couldn't imagine how she was going to explain this to her mom.

Alyeska dug in.

Another steep hill.

Tatum clung to the handlebars. "Cole!"

No answer.

Her team struggled along a ridge with turns that curved back on themselves. Tatum braced one boot against a bank on the downhill side, fighting to hang on, terrified of slipping and falling. It was impossible to keep her face turned away from the wind.

Don't panic, she told herself.

It wasn't about her—dogs ruled the snow.

Another hairpin turn. Snow was piled in deep drifts, some as tall as a barn. Alyeska kept them moving forward, taking the easiest route. The sled brushed Bandit, who still ran wheel dog. She whined, pricking her ears, speeding to keep from being crushed.

"Slow down!" Tatum stomped her brake. It grabbed, barely. She should have gone back! "Whoa! Not so fast!"

"Cole!" She shouted over a sudden gust, as it tried to drive her and Cole apart. Another gust and she fell off the sled, but didn't go all the way down. Her runners were instantly covered with snow and the soles of her boots were caked. She barely scrambled back on.

"Cole!" She desperately needed to stop and regroup.

The only response was a howling wind. No other sounds seemed to exist. Even her team was silent in their agony. Wind whipped up the snow, turning their dark fur white.

She'd heard endless stories of mushers getting stalled in whiteouts. Mushers who couldn't find trail markers and had to camp out. One guy hadn't zipped his sleeping bag all the

78

way. Wind had packed snow into every crevice. Hypothermia had set in overnight. A race official had found him half frozen and radioed for a medevac helicopter.

Tatum gripped the handlebars as another fist of wind rumbled at her from nowhere. Her shoulders screamed as she battled to keep her sled from flipping. This kind of wind usually brought foul weather.

Usually? No, it *always* did.

Two and a half years in Alaska had taught her that.

It shrieked louder, a warning.

Tatum knew she had to stop. Put Bandit in front. Bandit would have to be her eyes and ears—communicating wordlessly through her harness, down the line, into the sled and its handlebars, to Tatum.

She felt as if she was choking on snow instead of taking in air. It was cold, really cold. Wind scoured a patch of exposed skin where her neck gaiter had slipped.

Suddenly, the wind let up.

Tatum lifted her goggles and spotted Cole hunkered out of the wind in a gully not far away.

"Gee!" she hollered. She felt like she was riding on a sheet of tinfoil pulled by a speedboat. Alyeska brought her team to a shaky stop. Tatum stumbled downhill toward him.

"Dumb rookie move!" he said angrily, wrestling with his sled. It had slammed into an embankment. The ski pole had pierced a nasty hole in the canvas. He retaped it back in place. "Just so you know, we've been on a loop, heading back."

All she could see was white, white, white.

"How long will it take?" she asked.

"An hour max."

Tatum checked her watch. They'd already been gone three and a half hours. Dread filled her as she pictured her mom in the lodge, frantic with worry. She helped gather Cole's spilled gear and repack. Then she put Bandit back in the lead, breaking up a carrot for her.

It started snowing again, heavier than before. It swirled in a tsunami that crashed over the dogs. A second wave struck, harder than the first. Cole's parka spun in a void of nothingness. There wasn't even a tree to break up the expanse, as if she'd be able to see one.

Tatum tied down her hood, tightening her goggles. They were useless. Snow battered the lenses, building a sheet of ice. It was like looking through a horribly scratched window. Her lenses fogged. Her sled was a ghost. Her dogs phantoms. She was definitely in over her head.

Some mushers went crazy in whiteouts—attacking trees they mistook for giant monsters. Or seeing villages and freight trains that weren't there. *Hallucinations.* Lack of sleep made it worse. They'd doze on their sleds and dream of mushing, then wake up and see their dogs. After a while it was hard to know what was real and what wasn't.

She struggled for balance, fighting dizziness.

Visibility dropped to zero.

Vertigo.

It felt like she was whirling in space.

Needles of fear pricked her. She yanked at her goggles. Her eyelashes felt frozen. The temperature had dropped. If she stayed on the sled too long she'd risk frostbite. If she jogged beside it, her lungs could burn from the inside out. She was tired, disoriented.

It hurt to *think*.

Trust your gut. Be smart.

Cole appeared from nowhere, stumbling toward her. Bandit stopped, head down, panting. She was wet, her fur matted. Tatum had never seen a dog look so miserable. She cleared snow from Bandit's eyes.

"There's an old cabin," Cole shouted against the wind. "We can hole up till it blows over."

Tatum nodded, shielding her face with her gloves.

Before moving to Alaska she didn't know anything about blizzards. If it was stormy in Portland, she stayed inside. During the first fierce storm after they moved, her dad told her they were going out. "In this?" she'd asked, hoping he was kidding.

"How else will you learn?" he'd answered.

They'd headed out in their heaviest clothes, each holding one end of a four-foot-long rope. "So we won't get separated," her dad had said.

They'd come back after about forty minutes. Once inside, her dad asked her how far they'd walked. She guessed a mile. "We never made it to the woodpile," he'd said. That was less than a hundred feet from the house.

After the storm cleared, he showed her how to make an emergency snow cave. They tromped down snow on a short hill, then used shovels to dig in about four feet. "You need some kind of insulation for the floor," he'd told her. "That's really important."

"Okay," she'd said.

Just last month a record-breaking blizzard had grounded planes and ships. Trucks stayed in garages. *Now we're prisoners too*, Tatum thought.

Waiting it out sounded reasonable, so why did she feel so uneasy?

12

Cole worked the door against a bank of packed snow outside the cabin. If you could even call it a door. Bears had nearly totaled it. "Home, sweet home," he said with a crooked grin.

Was he kidding?

The cabin looked more like an oversized lettuce crate. Gasoline cans, hammered flat, were nailed over gaping holes. But four walls, no matter how sorry-looking, were better than fighting a storm. They'd never win. Besides, the dogs needed rest.

They shook snow from their coats. The colder it got, the faster water froze—and the faster it dried—just like wet laundry. But instead of sleeping, the dogs acted excited, like they were on a long vacation.

"Better unload the sleds," Cole shouted over the wind.

They moved feverishly without talking, wading through deep drifts, carting everything inside—snowshoes, shovel, ax, and a couple of thermal blankets. A sled was a type of mobile home.

Working helped take Tatum's mind off their nightmare. If she stopped moving, even for a nanosecond, cold seeped inside her clothes.

Cole lit a can of fuel. It burst into smoky flames. He shoveled snow into the cooker, watching it melt. Gradually the room warmed up enough for them to shed parkas and gloves. Tatum checked the dogs' feet, just like she did for Beryl, then helped feed and water them.

Bandit ate like a racehorse, making up for not finishing her breakfast. *Was that this morning?* It seemed like eons ago. Wolf picked at his food, leaving half of it on the moldy floor. Brooks and Denali jumped up, growling to see who'd get it.

Cole waved his glove. "Hey!"

The dogs shrank back.

He dropped two sealed bags into the simmering water, waited for them to thaw, then passed Tatum a steaming bag. "Homemade chili."

She took it, grateful for a hot meal. "Thanks."

"No one predicted this storm." He said it like an apology.

Tatum started to reply, but thought better of it. Nothing she could say would change their grim situation.

She sat on an upended crate, eating chili from the bag— that was how Beryl ate on the trail, so she wouldn't have to wash dishes. Ziplock bags were good for all kinds of things. Mittens or socks, in a pinch. Beryl once made an emergency rain poncho from a plastic garbage bag.

Tatum took in the sight: Bandit, Brooks, Chugach, Kenai, Alyeska, and Wrangell, Cole's lead dog, curled up and asleep. Bandit looked like she was winking. Tatum smiled; even Wolf seemed content.

Cole opened the door to a blustering wind. It was loud enough to be heard in Nome. *Is it ever going to let up?*

He dragged both sleds inside, blowing on his red fingers. A halo of light from the flames shone on his torn basket.

"No one knows we're here," she finally said.

He took out dental floss and a needle large enough to suture a whale. "Standard repair equipment," he said, and made a big, looping stitch.

After a while, Tatum took over. She finished the job with a knot. "Will someone be looking for us?"

"This summer I'm working with kids—teaching them our language and customs," he said instead of answering her. "When I shot my first seal, my mother threw a party. We divided the meat and blubber among everyone in the village. I stood outside our door giving away gifts of seal oil, rice, and toilet paper.

"The village kids need survival skills. If it comes from someone younger—not just the elders—maybe they'll listen. It's happened in other villages."

"Why don't you just say it?" she snapped at him, tired of being ignored. "We're stuck here overnight."

13

Tatum awoke stiff and sore, feeling like she'd spent the night in a rock tumbler. Bandit slept next to her, warm as toast. Tatum's stomach grumbled. There wasn't much trail mix left. And the supply of dog food was dangerously low. She'd rather eat snow than touch what they'd brought for the dogs. Not that dog food, turkey skin, or whale blubber sounded appetizing.

Cole was buried in his sleeping bag.

She checked her watch: 6:42 a.m. Nearly twenty-four hours had passed since they'd left Wager. How had it gotten so late? Even if the storm cleared they couldn't make it back in time for the flight to Nome. She was really in for it now!

Tatum scooted out of her sleeping bag and tugged on her boots. She fought to open the door, praying for sun. A solid white wall blocked their exit. She couldn't tell how thick it was.

Cole made a noise and opened his eyes. He yawned noisily and looked around as if he didn't know where he was. Then he saw the wall of snow. "I'll get my ax," he said, kicking out of his bag.

Tatum built a fire in an oil drum that had been sawed in half. It was elevated off the ground by a metal frame, like the one on the deck at Skilak Lodge. Only there she'd helped barbecue chicken and moose steaks for guests. She found matches in a plastic bag and squirted kindling with Blazo. Thankfully, hunters kept the place stocked with basics. Like a row of dominoes in reverse, the dogs stood up, shaking themselves off.

Wrangell gnawed on his bootie like it was a chew toy. Wolf hunkered in the corner, watching Bandit. Bandit ignored him, wagging her tail, ready to get going.

"The dogs can have the rest of the whale blubber," Cole said.

Feeding the dogs didn't take Tatum's mind off being hungry, until Wolf threw up. "He ate too fast," Cole said.

Tatum hoped he wasn't getting sick. "You okay, fella?"

Wolf growled.

She kicked straw over the mess.

Cole kept hacking away at the snow until there was a tunnel wide enough to crawl through. He stopped to rest, looking exhausted. He sat on a crate and took off his beanie and wet gloves. His hands were white and shriveled, his black hair plastered flat. "No wind," he mumbled.

Tatum stirred cocoa into mugs of hot water. She handed one to him.

"The snow—" he said, and took a noisy slurp. "It'd take a bulldozer to plow through it. There's a creek nearby. . . . The footing will be firmer. Faster too."

"But it's March," she said, worried about overflow ice.

Cole watched Alyeska and Denali chase each other through the tunnel, as if it had been dug for their amusement. "Ice doesn't thaw this far inland for another month or more."

Tatum dumped water from the cooker into the fire drum. The last of the coals sizzled and died. She heard a rumbling sound, and part of the tunnel collapsed. Alyeska and Denali barked, barely escaping.

Cole swore and grabbed his ax.

Tatum picked up the shovel.

● ● ●

The snow outside the cabin looked so new, so clean, not a bootprint or any other sign of life. The bluster had blown itself out; the blinding brightness was harsh in a different way. No matter what the conditions, the dogs rarely got discouraged.

They packed up quickly.

Then Cole wandered off. Tatum didn't ask where he was going. Guys had it easy in the outdoors when it came to personal business. Tatum looked for a private spot.

She came back, finished packing, and put Bandit in the lead.

Bandit licked her nose, happy to get going.

Tatum and Cole walked in front of their teams to help blaze a trail. The dogs sank shoulder-deep with every step.

"It'd be easier to carry them," she muttered, worn out all over again.

Cole released the tuglines so his dogs could run without shouldering any weight. Half an hour later he rehitched them. It was Bandit's turn to break trail. Cole's team followed. Tatum rode up a steep knoll, only to discover that their path was blocked. The dogs hated backtracking.

The wind had swept clean patches, making the next stretch slick and fast.

Tatum struggled to keep her sled from slamming into the steep sides. The dogs struggled to keep their footing. Booties fell off. They didn't stop to pick them up. The sound of scraping sled runners filled the morning air. She tried to remember a time when she had thought this was fun.

Grandfather had to know about the cabin—that they would have spent the night there. Tatum listened for an engine, a plane, or, more likely, a snowmobile. Thoughts of being rescued flooded her head.

They climbed another steep crest. The creek twisted below, a frozen rope speckled with fog. Cole's team slowed halfway to the bank. "Better snack the dogs," he called to her.

Tatum helped check harnesses and replace lost booties. Both teams were antsy, sniffing the air like it held a secret. Cole swapped Wrangell and Alyeska. When it was time to get going, Wolf spanked the ground with his tail, refusing to get up. Cole tried coaxing him.

"Maybe he's sick," Tatum said.

Cole looked uncertain, then dragged Wolf to the sled and heaved him inside.

They took off again.

Soon they were in the heavy fog, solid and low. The fog reminded Tatum of Portland. Every year dense fog caused car wrecks, closed freeways. It was so thick you could reach out and grab it.

The wind kicked up, howling from the west, straight from the sea. Tatum yanked up her face mask, thinking that everything that could go wrong had. Now fog *and* wind. She wondered how that was possible. Then a gust caught her basket.

We can survive the cold, but the wind will be the end of us!

Her team zigzagged to keep from getting hit head-on by the wind. Cole's sled slowed, partly because Wolf was inside. That and the loss of muscle power in his team.

To keep from going crazy she thought about camping last summer with her dad . . . crackling bonfires . . . pan-fried fish . . . *s'mores!* She thought about Skilak Lodge . . . counting bald eagles . . . picking berries. Grizzlies loved berries. Her dad taught her to sing or wear bells on her boots so they'd hear her coming. He said bears avoided people whenever possible.

She kept moving.

The fog finally lifted and the wind died. The sun sparkled on the creek, turning it into a blanket of diamonds. They stopped and dropped their hooks. Wolf lifted his head from the sled, sniffing the clean air.

Tatum pushed back her hood. Bareheaded, she felt her

tangled hair slapping her in the face. She hooked it behind her ears. Everywhere she looked snow was piled high. Spirits of the native people Grandfather had talked about seemed everywhere and nowhere.

Cole pulled a half-eaten Baby Ruth from his parka. "I wonder how long that's been in there. Better save it."

Tatum nodded. Rationing food was a reality check on how little they had left.

14

A blaze of sunlight drew Tatum's gaze up the slope where a caribou and her calf stood shoulder deep in snow. Their legs were as skinny as Cole's ski pole.

"Why aren't they with the herd?" she asked.

"Parasites."

Last summer she'd seen a young moose covered by so many mosquitoes it looked like it was wearing a thick blanket. "Mosquitoes are winged vampires," she said, quoting her dad.

"Know why there aren't any snakes on the island?" Cole asked.

"Mosquitoes ate them."

That got a smile out of him. "Gnats and blackflies are worse," he said.

They took off again.

The frozen creek changed colors at every bend. Sometimes the ice was as dark as coal; other times a shimmery blue-green. Farther on, the snow on the frozen creek was deeper, but not deep enough to slow them down.

Tatum thought her sled sounded different. It even felt different. She squinted at the glare magnified by the endless whiteness and let herself drift into autopilot.

The creek curved back toward a wind-blasted plateau, narrowed for a snaky stretch, then widened again. She followed Cole along the shoreline. "We'll stop around the next bend!" he hollered. "Regroup!"

And that was just what Bandit did, right then.

Stopped in the middle of the creek.

"Not here, girl," Tatum said.

Bandit looked over her shoulder, tongue hanging out, holding back. She went a short way, faltered, slowed, and stopped again.

"Get up there!" Cole shouted.

Bandit dropped her head, laying back her ears.

"Come on, now!" Tatum echoed. Bandit had never acted like this last summer. Why now? "Hike!" she hollered.

Her dog took another cautious step, then hesitated. She dug in stubbornly.

"Make her do what you tell her," Cole snapped.

Tatum stiffened, unable to shake a sudden feeling of dread. "What if she's sick? Like Wolf?"

"Put Alyeska in front," he said.

Tatum rushed to the head of her team and lined them out straight. In her haste she couldn't get Alyeska's tugline resnapped to the mainline. Her fingers weren't cooperating; her mind wasn't either. She should be taking her time. *Right!*

93

"Hurry up," Cole said, losing patience.

"I'm doing the best I can!" she shouted back.

"Before the creek thaws!"

Tatum finally got the dogs switched.

"Follow me!" Cole called.

Tatum's team moved so slowly it seemed like they were backing up. Bandit tugged against the line, slowing them even more. Then the whole team started acting up. Suddenly they veered right and booked it for the bank.

Alyeska stayed close to Cole's sled. Both teams worked their way over an expanse where the snow wasn't as deep. They edged a ridge that made a steep climb. From the top it was a sharp downhill turn along a narrow ravine.

"Hold on!" Cole called back. "This could get hairy!"

Tatum tightened her grip, trying to breathe evenly. She timed her breaths with Bandit's gait. Her goggles dug into her face. They were too tight. Within seconds she had a screaming headache.

They zigzagged around willows, squat shrubs shaped by fierce winds. They ticked off a couple of hard-fought miles and moved uphill along the high bank of a river, then veered downhill again. The route twisted with endless ruts and bumps.

That was when she heard it.

The unmistakable sound of cracking ice.

Tatum stopped, choking on a breath. Her brain didn't know what to do—what to think—how to process what her eyes were seeing. They'd been running on a river without even knowing it.

A section of ice caved in on itself. "No!" she cried out.

The dogs went wild, pulling against the lines. Wolf barked from inside the sled. Another crack. *Crash!* Raft-sized jags of ice tilted upward. One hitched a ride on the other.

Ice shifted, tilted, bobbed.

The river was chaotic, shattering into countless islands. Her dogs flailed in their harnesses.

Bandit had known it. She'd heard water below the ice, maybe even smelled it. That was why she'd stopped.

"Follow me!" Cole sounded frantic. He was actually shaking in his boots. He threaded his way around an open lane of water, desperately searching for a safe path to shore.

We're sledding through a deadly maze, Tatum thought. *This is what happens to people who drift onto the frozen sea, and their ice island slowly melts inch by inch until there's nothing left.*

Stupid thoughts! She had to push them from her mind or she'd go insane. But she couldn't ignore the thunderous cracks, like the roar of a horrible monster. The din echoed beneath her boots, freight cars bumping into each other, hooking and unhooking.

She forced herself to concentrate on her dogs. "Easy now." She encouraged them as they inched forward, heads down. "Easy there."

Cole's route had to be safe. Otherwise he would have already broken through the ice. Then suddenly ice was attacking them from all directions. The flood of killing water came from all sides.

Tatum screamed. She couldn't help it. She imagined her team being dragged under, ice closing over them like a deadly lid. The pressure of the grinding floes could take a dogsled and crush it like an eggshell.

Stop it!

They struggled a few yards, only to discover a break too wide to cross. They stopped, retraced their route. The dogs howled. They fought to balance on the shifting ice. Booties were torn off. Claws scraped ice.

Tatum's heart pounded in her ears. Her head ached. She shoved back her goggles. "There are times on the trail when nothing makes sense," Beryl had told her last summer. "When it seems like you're traveling in a parallel universe."

Another section of ice buckled.

If she survived this she'd never be the same.

Cole's team squeezed around a fissure.

Tatum spotted a narrow ice bridge. "Is it strong enough?" she called.

Cole stopped and studied the confusion of jagged up-thrusts. They looked solid enough, but underneath was a treacherous crevasse. "It's impossible to know how deep it is," he said.

A frozen plug was hammering the ice bridge. Every second grew colder, the shadows longer. She tried not to look down. Hypothermia, the killing cold of the north.

Her dad said it didn't take long for body temperature to plunge from the normal 98.6 to 95 degrees. Further drops, and the heart rate decreased. Finally, the most important organs—lungs, kidney, brain—simply shut down.

People need built-in antifreeze, she thought fiercely, *like animals that hibernate.*

"Is there another way?"

Cole shook his head. He stepped off his sled and tilted it onto a single runner.

Tatum watched him move forward.

Then the unthinkable happened.

In a swirl of confusion, Wolf scrambled from Cole's sled. He leaped over an open channel and bounded for shore. Wrangell and Denali fought the lines, trying to follow. They slipped and splashed headfirst into the freezing water. "Wrangell!" Cole shouted desperately. "Tatum! Set the hook!"

She was paralyzed by the sight of the sinking dogs. *They're going to die.* Wrangell howled wildly, trying to claw his way onto the ice. The sound was horrible.

"Set the hook!" Cole repeated, frantic to save his team.

Tatum shook herself free. She slammed the snow hook into the ice, unsure how long the anchor would hold, then grabbed the gangline in a deadly tug-of-war. Her on one side, two drowning dogs on the other.

"Get the ax!" Cole struggled to keep his lead dog from going under. "Cut the line!"

Tatum clutched the ax and hacked furiously. She'd reached her limit, her brain played out. "The nylon . . . it's . . . I can't cut it!"

"Just do it!"

She slammed down with all her strength. One strike, then another. Bandit let out a deep-throated bark. *I'm losing my battle with this nightmare.* But she couldn't give up. She kept raising the ax and slamming it down, until the line frayed; then, *Snap!*

Cole fell backward on his butt. Wrangell and Denali scrambled to shore, dragging the rest of the team, their dark eyes crazy with fear.

Tatum staggered back to her sled. She gave a kick, and her team flew over what was left of the collapsing ice bridge.

15

Brooks and Alyeska stood shivering on the bank. Cole grabbed a blanket and rubbed them furiously. Wolf paced the uneven slope, his shoulders hunched. "Bandit," Cole said, as if he couldn't believe it. "She's one smart dog. None of mine knew we were on overflow ice—not even Wrangell."

Bandit yipped, like she understood.

Tatum didn't answer. She was doubled over, afraid she was going to be sick, and this time she was. She shuddered, wiping her mouth on her sleeve. She coughed, her throat raw with cold. Her bottom lip stung.

They had survived. She let that fill her with hope. Then another sheet of ice buckled and the area where they had been standing filled with killing water. *That could have been us!*

"Fire up the cooker," Cole commanded.

Tatum pulled the pot from his sled and began shoveling snow, wondering how long the weather would hold. Bandit stayed on her like a shadow. "I wish we had logs for a real fire," Tatum said to herself.

On an island without trees? Not a chance.

The dogs lapped up the meager meal with satisfied growls: hot water with chicken fat and turkey skins mixed in. Not much nutrition. But it was warm and kept them hydrated.

Wolf got his appetite back, along with his nasty temperament. He snarled at anything that moved, especially Tatum.

"Knock it off!" Cole growled back, smacking him on the head.

Wolf tucked his tail between his legs and retreated.

Tatum slumped beside the cooker. "Did you have to do that?"

"He's too stubborn to learn any other way." Cole dragged Wolf by his harness and staked him away from the others.

Cole came over to warm his hands. He stared at the quilt of sleeping dogs. Just one big furry patchwork, piled up to stay warm. "They need a good hour before we go on," he said.

Tatum shared the last of the pretzels with him. They tasted like sawdust, and barely took the edge off her hunger. She licked her cracked lips, tasted blood, uncapped her beeswax. The sun was dropping fast, like it was in a hurry. *What are we going to do?*

"The dogs need solid food. Meat," Cole said, cutting into her thoughts. "They aren't starving, yet. . . ."

His words punched her. "What does that mean?"

"You've heard of Admiral Byrd?" His eyes were on the breathing pile. "And his expedition to the South Pole?"

Tatum shifted uncomfortably.

"Know why they took so many dogs?" Now he turned to face her.

It was probably the same reason mushers started the Iditarod with twice as many dogs as they needed to finish. "In case some of them got hurt or sick?"

"They couldn't transport enough dog food," he said slowly. "Not for a whole year. If a dog got sick they sacrificed it, to feed the stronger ones."

Tatum glared at him. "You can shut up right now."

Cole glared right back. "It's history."

"*Ancient* history." No way she'd let Cole touch one of these dogs. He could eat her first. "And it's *cannibalism*."

"Grandfather hooked thirty-six dogs to his house," he said, looking away. "They towed it more than a hundred and seventy-five miles across the ice, from Anvil to Wager."

Tatum knew all about sled dogs and their strength. But what was his point?

Cole walked over to the dogs, calling them by name. Only Denali raised his head, sniffing for food. When he didn't see any he tucked a paw over his nose.

Cole grabbed his harness. "Come on, it's time to go."

Denali went limp.

"Up!"

The other dogs watched, but didn't budge. Except Wolf, who raced around his stake, tangling his line and nearly choking himself.

Tatum knew it was impossible to force a team to run when they were worn out. It happened in the Iditarod too. Sometimes teams just refused to get up after a layover. "They need more rest," she said.

Cole knew it. He stomped off to untangle Wolf.

Tatum turned her sled on its side and butted it against an embankment. Cole came back and pulled a deerskin hide from his sled. He spread it on the ground, hair-side down. "Can you rig up some kind of roof?"

Tatum switched on her headlamp, hating the way it dug into her chapped skin. But it was getting dark fast. She looked around for something she could use as a tie-down. She found a piece of cord and used it to secure a sheet of canvas over the two sleds.

She admired her work, thinking her dad would approve, then realized there wasn't any way to get inside. *If brains were fish guts, I'd never stink!*

She quickly untied a corner and folded it back. The makeshift shelter was good enough for two people for the night. Tatum headed over to the dogs, shining her light on the lumps.

Bandit had settled in with the others, looking snug under a blanket of snow. Tatum bent down and kissed the top of her head. "Good night, girl."

Bandit yawned and licked her nose.

Tatum wiped it off before it could freeze.

Now she stood over the cramped space, the beam of her headlamp shining on the deerskin floor. She crawled inside and struggled out of her boots, snow pants, wet parka. Long underwear and wool socks would be warm enough inside a sleeping bag.

Cole settled in on his side, stooping under the low roof. He bundled up his outer clothes to keep moisture from seeping in. "An old Eskimo trick," he said. He reached up and closed the flap.

Tatum switched off her headlamp and shoved it deep in her bag so the battery wouldn't freeze. She scooted into her sleeping bag, yanking on the zipper until her fingers nearly fell off, then put on wool mittens. She used her parka for a pillow, breathing into her fur ruff. It radiated back like a heater.

"Don't worry," Cole said. "Grandfather knows we're safe. He'll talk to your mom."

Every cell in her body wanted to believe it. But this was their second night out here. Her mom would be a basket case no matter what Grandfather said.

A while later, Cole peeled back a corner of the roof. "Some people think those are stars," he said, eyes skyward. "But they're really holes so our ancestors can smile down to let us know they're happy."

Tatum tried to imagine it. "Or lights to guide weary travelers," she said.

"Like the red lantern in the Iditarod."

Cole was quiet for a long time before he spoke again. "We'll chop a hole in the sea ice."

He's talking about a breathing hole for a seal.

"The dogs need meat," he said. "Fat."

Tatum listened to the wind whip through the darkness.

She and her dad had been fishing more times than she could count. She'd helped him gut fish. They had roasted filets over a crackling fire and picked meat off the bones. She'd seen locals gut fish by tromping on them with a boot. The insides shot out the mouth and were saved for bait. But *seals*?

Tatum sank deeper in her bag. She didn't think she'd been asleep, but she awoke with a start and realized she'd been dreaming about summer at Skilak Lodge. She drifted off again and slept so hard she awakened in the same position. The lumpy ground poked at her. Every muscle ached.

Tired as she was after two long days out here, she rolled onto her side—eyes and ears adjusting to the dark—and peeked out. The dogs slept soundly, tails curled to noses. She looked up the slope where Wolf was staked. He was standing up, shoulders bulging, head forward. Snow dusted his wiry coat.

Why aren't you asleep?

He looked enormous, standing there alone. He lifted his nose to the wind, his head blocking out the moon, and howled.

The sky was sprinkled with stars. Not a snowflake anywhere. The wind had died down, but the air was still electric. Tatum was about to lie back when a kaleidoscope of yellowish green streaked overhead—wispy fountains swirled across the sky. Then streamers exploded in blue violet, flickering off the sleeping dogs.

She lay there, very still, watching the light show. There were many legends about the northern lights. *Aurora borealis*. One said the lights were torches held by spirits who were looking for the souls of people who had died recently. Others claimed the sweeps of color had healing powers. She imagined spirits dancing on stars.

Somewhere beyond the bank, she heard ice move in the river. It sounded like a monster thrashing in its bed. She rolled over and dozed. After an hour of fitful sleep, she sat up with a jolt. Her stomach rumbled. She was too aware of being cold and hungry—and of the dogs' need for food.

Cole stirred. "Is it light?"

Tatum's hair felt dirty, her face raw and chapped. "Yeah, and it's clear."

Cole struggled to untie the rest of their roof. His fingers were red and puffy. "H-E-double-hockey-sticks!" He swore when a pile of snow fell on him.

Tatum had a tough time convincing her body it was time to get up. She forced herself to put on her outer gear and checked her thermometer. Sun pulsated on the snow, but the temperature hovered around zero. She helped Cole roll up the deerskin rug.

"We have some blubber left," he said. "And half a stale candy bar."

Each lump of dog stood up and stretched. Bandit yawned and shook her fur clean of snow.

Cole fired up the cooker and hacked the blubber into smaller pieces. Tatum didn't bother asking about their route back. She knew they'd be taking the shortest way to the beach to hunt for seals.

They finished mugs of watery cocoa and the last bites of trail mix before packing up. Bandit raced around the sled, barking. She wanted the lead. Tatum gave it to her.

Wolf was better, and back on Cole's line. He ran with his

head down, constantly nosing the ground. It took a few miles for the dogs to loosen up and find their stride. The snow was deep, choppy—an endless tract they were forced to deal with to get someplace else.

Tatum felt the strain of every curve. It took more fuel to keep a body going in this kind of cold. Even wearing two pairs of wool socks, she stamped her boots every time she could. She slipped heat packs inside her gloves and tightened her goggles.

She couldn't remember ever being so tired. The more tired she became, the more she worried about her sled hitting a hidden chunk of ice. It wouldn't take much to knock her off her feet. For the first time since they'd left the village, she wished someone else could take care of her dogs.

Will this ever end? she wondered, losing all track of time.

16

Bandit stayed on Cole's heels where the snow was smoother. She looked cold and miserable too, bracing against the sudden gusts. "Hang in there," Tatum cooed to her.

Bandit wagged her tail halfheartedly.

A wind blowing forty miles an hour could batter everything in its path, Tatum knew from a bizarre math teaser. Especially dogs trying to keep a sled straight. At zero degrees a dog could stand in one place, get slammed with a chill factor of minus seventy degrees, and still survive.

She could see for herself that wind had created impassable drifts in places that should have been easy going. It blew so hard the dry snow on top disappeared.

It's like a white Dust Bowl, Tatum thought. *We're in some freaky race against the weather*.

The third morning fell away in steep bends and unrelenting wind. More drifts piled up.

They kept on.

Hours slipped by.

Gusts hit sixty miles per hour. At least, that was her guess.

Bandit crept along, her tail down.

It's okay, girl, Tatum willed through the lines.

It was impossible to prepare for this kind of wind. Every mile was agony. Tatum felt like a five-foot-tall snowball being blown down the trail. Worry nudged her; she knew the dogs were losing moisture with every breath.

Cole stopped and set his hook. He rushed back to make sure everything on her sled was tied down.

"We're losing time!" she shouted.

He couldn't hear her.

She reached out and caught her loose mitten as it flew past.

Cole hurried back to his team and kept going.

He missed a turn that jagged abruptly to the right. His sled whipped around, out of control and spinning like a kicked bottle.

"Cole!" She watched him stumble over the bank. He landed face-first in a tangle of dogs.

Tatum didn't wait to set her hook. She rushed down the slope, sinking knee-deep in snow. She fought to keep her boots from being sucked off her feet. "Are you okay?"

Cole's cheek was badly scraped and bleeding. Hoarfrost glazed his eyebrows. He scooped snow and pressed it against his face. He looked completely beaten down.

"I'll untangle the dogs," she said.

Tatum did the best she could to straighten out Cole's team, then got to work on his sled. The weight of his gear had pushed it deep into the snow. She needed the shovel, but it had sunk with everything else. She dug with her hands, her shoulders aching.

The wind died, but the sky was clear and cold. Silence grew into a sound of its own, settling over them like a slab of rock. The dogs napped, sprawled in their harnesses. Except Wolf, who watched Tatum intently, looking hungry enough to swallow her in one bite. *Why doesn't he like me?*

Cole helped pull his sled the rest of the way out. He frowned at a wide crack in the runner. "Can't go far on that," he said, shaking his head miserably. His cheek looked nasty.

Tatum watched him tape a snowshoe to the runner like a splint. When everything was lashed down, he jerked on the gangline. Only two of his dogs got up; Wrangell and Chugach held back. Cole didn't try coaxing them. He put Wrangell inside his sled, Chugach inside Tatum's.

Bandit looked over her shoulder, tail drooping, as if thinking, *Another fifty pounds?*

"Sorry, girl." Tatum wished there was another way.

Bandit couldn't find her usual rhythm. She strained, lunging in heaving steps over the next ridge. First Wolf, then Wrangell and Chugach. Tatum kept an eye on Bandit, afraid she'd be next. Sometimes it seemed like adrenaline pumped nothing but fear through her body.

Another ridge, and she dragged the brake. She swapped Bandit with Alyeska. It took longer than usual, nearly ten minutes. The dogs barked the whole time, begging for a snack. Cole divided the last of the frozen turkey skin. Bandit left her piece between her paws.

Tatum tried coaxing her. "Come on, girl. You have to eat."

Bandit moved it around with her nose.

"Maybe I should heat it?" she asked Cole.

He shrugged, which meant *Forget it*.

Suddenly, Denali bristled. In one leap he was on Bandit. Tatum screamed, "Hey!"

Cole grabbed Denali before the other dogs could get into the mix. Bandit cowered, rolling on her back, pawing the air. Tatum kneeled beside her, light-headed. "It's okay," she said, stroking her.

But it wasn't okay. Denali had stolen Bandit's snack. The turkey skin was gone; so was all the blubber. All they had left was a small bag of dry food. For eight dogs? No way.

Denali was usually so mellow. Now he was willing to attack for a measly scrap of skin. The other dogs would have joined in. Tatum tried to make sense of it. Instinct, like a pack of wolves smelling the kill. That was how insane it was getting out here.

Food.

No fish. No birds. No eggs.

Not even a lemming. As kids, Tatum's dad and his friends had trapped the small, mouselike rodents. "When food is scarce," he'd told her, "they migrate in furry masses. After reaching the sea, they swim a short distance and drown. What a sad sight."

Tatum had to remember where she was. She had to stay attuned to the dogs—all the dogs. Poor Bandit. She wrapped her arms around Bandit's neck. Bandit nibbled her face mask. Thoughts of what might have happened if all the dogs had attacked filled every space in Tatum's body.

Back on the trail, she felt the extra weight in her sled every time they turned a corner. It tipped twice, almost going over. Chugach whined constantly. Wrangell chewed through another bootie. Bandit ran with her head down, nipping snow, her tail swishing.

The snowshoe taped to Cole's sled made it look like it was limping. Under different circumstances Tatum would have thought it was funny. Another hour passed.

Cole let his claw brake drag. "Better rest awhile," he said.

Tatum nodded, throwing down her hook. A young caribou stood on a slope not far away. His ribs and hips stuck out and his thick coat was matted. He raised and lowered his head awkwardly, obviously sick. The dogs sniffed the wind.

Tatum unhooked Bandit, holding on to the harness. She was about to put her behind Denali, when Bandit jerked away and charged the caribou. "No!" Tatum cried, her stomach clenching. "Come back!"

Cole grabbed her sleeve. "Let her go."

Shaking free, Tatum slipped into an unreal movie. Bandit floated through the air as some ancient impulse took over. The yearling stared, eyes bulging, fear-struck. Bandit sank her teeth into his scrawny neck. The caribou barely struggled before going down. Bandit held on. Then it was over.

Tatum sank inside herself, unable to move. Her throat closed. Even sick, the caribou had been beautiful. His eyes were still open, staring. His white tail looked like a flag of surrender. The other dogs were going crazy, slamming against their harnesses. They chomped at the air, dying for a taste of blood.

They're starving, she thought. *Bandit's starving*. Cole was right. It was nature's way. The yearling would have died on his own, and the meat would have been wasted.

Tatum closed her eyes to the terrible sight.

I will not cry.

17

Cole pulled his ulu from its leather sheath, making it impossible not to acknowledge the caribou's death. What had happened was not some kind of bizarre dream. With the knife's curved blade glinting, Cole slit the hide from the neck, down the chest, and over the belly. He started peeling it back, a few inches at a time.

"Sick animals understand why they're taken," he said, working slowly. "They know they're going to a greater good."

Tatum looked away, worrying about the dogs. She wondered if they could get sick from eating a sick animal.

Then she turned back, forcing herself to watch. Otherwise she'd never be at home in the wild.

Her stomach turned while Cole pushed, pulled, lifted, skinned, and twisted joints. He ignored the blood. Bandit paced around the carcass. Wrangell and Chugach had jumped from the sleds. But they stayed back, away from the kill. The tethered dogs howled, impatient for their share. Wolf's ears were forward, waiting.

"Nothing is wasted—not the heart, lungs, tongue." Cole leaned over the belly and pulled out steaming guts. "The elders teach us to treat animals with respect when we butcher them so their spirits will return for a future harvest."

Cole sliced off a chunk of yellowish fat and cut it into smaller pieces. He threw Bandit the first fistful and tossed the rest to the other dogs. They growled, snatching it up hungrily. Wolf ate it so fast, he threw up, then ate it again.

Tatum wrapped her arms around herself. She couldn't ignore what was happening. There was so much blood, so much meat. She couldn't imagine how much there would have been if the yearling had been healthy and full-grown.

"He died quietly, without the roar of a rifle," Cole said. He cut strips of red meat and bigger hunks that looked like roasts. "I bet you think the old ways are strange."

"No," she said. "Not strange."

"Grandfather eats the eyes. I don't like them, though. Too rubbery."

She shook her head. "Think I'll pass too."

Tatum watched Cole dig a pit in the snow, taking in what he was saying and how he was saying it. Then he started singing. She liked the melody and the sound of the words, and wished she knew what they meant.

Bandit yipped a song of her own, rising and falling. The others chimed in. A doggy symphony.

Tatum stood up and took a cautious step forward. The ground felt unsteady. Step by step, she focused on the twisted shape lying on the ground. It wasn't fair to let Cole do all the work.

Slowly, she gripped a leg. It felt solid in her hands, warm and damp through her gloves. She dragged it to the pit. Blood streaked the snow. Her breath worked its way under her goggles. They fogged up. She started to wipe them with her gloves, but those were soaked too.

Cole butchered a carload of meat, constantly tossing chunks to the dogs. They ate and ate and ate. Then they slept, worn out from so much food. He chopped a steak off a hind leg and added it to the hot water in the cooker.

"Thank you for the meat, caribou," he said quietly. The smell of cooking meat swirled around them. "You saved our lives."

Tatum lowered her head, grateful for solid food. Their conversations were shorter now. She chewed and choked down the stringy meat. The juice was both sweet and salty. She tried not to think about where it came from.

A Styrofoam tray wrapped in plastic, she told herself. Like chicken breasts and pork chops from the market in Nome.

They put the butchered meat inside the canvas tarp. Cole added the head; the eyes were still open.

By then the soup had cooled. Cole skimmed off the fat for the dogs and poured it into a container for later. Tatum forced herself to eat until the hollow feeling in her stomach disappeared. She hated the taste in her mouth. *What I'd give for a toothbrush!*

Cole shoveled snow over the pit, marking the temporary

freezer with his ski pole. Then he showed Tatum how to glaze her runners with ice. "A glassy surface slides best on this kind of snow," he explained.

Tatum glanced from dog to dog. With full bellies all were eager to run, all except . . . Where was Bandit? She shaded her eyes and shouted, "Bandit!"

"She probably dragged off a bone," Cole said.

Tatum looked around, unsettled. "I shouldn't have left her loose."

She walked toward the wind-blasted plateau, shouting until her throat ached. "Bandit!" She stopped, slowly turning a circle. Everything was quiet. She searched on, her boots barely skimming the snow. Why would Bandit run off like this? Unless . . . Had she gotten sick from eating the caribou?

Cole shouted after her. "Tatum! It isn't safe to take off on your own!"

"I have to find Bandit!" she shouted back.

Cole took a few steps, then turned back to his dogs.

She felt faint, unable to shake the feeling that something terrible had happened. "Bandit!" She wasn't focused on anything but finding her dog. "Where are you!"

Tatum knew she needed to calm down. She stumbled onto a ledge that cut straight down to the riverbank and dropped to her knees. Below she saw a speck of black and cinnamon. "Bandit!"

Wind swept her words away.

Just as suddenly the vision disappeared. A chill shot through her, and she slipped into some dark hole. Then back out of it. She tried desperately to think, pulling herself to her feet. She pictured the way Bandit looked at her, the way she reached up and licked her face.

She trudged to the edge of a ravine and a low-hanging shelf of ice. Underneath, dug into the bank, something moved.

Suddenly the air filled with a short, piercing yelp. It was the worst sound she'd ever heard, like someone being ripped in two. She cut down the slope, light-headed with adrenaline. Her heart pounded. She saw a thin line of blood splattered in the snow. "Bandit!"

Bandit peeked out from a shallow bed dug into the shelf. She was stone-still, out of the wind, trying to blend in. Tatum gulped for air and stumbled on. Bandit raised her head, quivering and breathing in short gasps. She was shaking all over.

Tatum knelt down, staring into her dog's tired eyes. "What's wrong, girl?" she cooed in a whisper. "What's the matter? Are you sick?"

Bandit looked different. Smaller somehow, weak. She raised her head and shook frost from her whiskers. Tatum stroked her head over and over. "It'll be okay," she repeated, wanting to believe it. Then she saw a tiny black ball. And another one, wet and shiny. Three in all, clamped to Bandit's teats.

Puppies?

The word *puppies* kept rattling in her head.

Puppies!

18

Bandit nuzzled her new family.

"They look like crushed velvet," Tatum said softly to herself.

She remembered Beryl's words: "Bandit hasn't been herself lately."

Wait until she hears about this!

Ice crystals swirled like fine sugar, floating around the snowy bed. The puppies must have been born right away. They had been cleaned up by the time Tatum found them.

Tatum was thinking three puppies was a tiny litter when a fourth one appeared. When it didn't move at first, she did the only thing she could think of. She quickly wiped away the membrane, and was relieved when the wet ball stirred.

"You're okay, little guy." She nuzzled him against her

neck, feeling his warm breath before setting him beside the others.

Bandit licked him head to toe, nudging him toward warm milk. Tatum settled on her heels, cooing to her dog. She'd never seen anything like this before. Bandit cocked her head, smiling and letting herself be petted.

Tatum did her best to explain what had to be done. "You'll be warm as wool in my sled," she said. "You have to trust me, okay?"

Bandit flashed her doggy smile again.

One by one, Tatum lifted the puppies, nestling them inside her parka. Bandit got to her feet, and slowly they made their way back.

Cole met them halfway. "Puppies?" He looked dumbstruck.

"I can't believe it either," Tatum said.

"Beryl didn't know?" he asked.

She shook her head. "No."

"Four's a small litter." He ushered them back to camp, opened a thermal blanket, and spread it out on the bottom of Tatum's sled. He lifted Bandit as carefully as if lifting a sleeping baby.

Tatum set the four puppies beside their mother. The family was reunited. Safe, warm, happy. Only Alyeska sniffed the sled curiously.

Cole shooed him away.

Tatum stared at the miracle. It really was unbelievable. *Puppies*. Out here in the frozen wilderness.

She knew Cole was exhausted by the way he moved. He

seemed different too. Something Tatum couldn't pin down. She watched him fish stringy meat from the cooker with his knife.

His cheek looked bad, bruised and swelling. "Wolf's gone." He said it flatly, his eyes on her.

"What do you mean?"

"Guess he'd rather be a lone wolf than run with a pack of dogs."

Tatum stared at him as the reality of their situation sank in. Bandit couldn't pull. Chugach and Brooks were sick. That left Kenai, Alyeska, Wrangell, and Denali. Four dogs couldn't pull two sleds, one of them with a broken runner. Not towing three dogs, two mushers, gear, and a caribou carcass.

"How far is it to Anvil?" She shifted, afraid of the answer.

The flicker from the cooker burned in Cole's eyes.

He looked away.

The moment hung.

"One of us has to wait here," she said, knowing she was right. "Is that it?"

His silence was a hundred times worse than if he'd been shouting. He must have been thinking about it while she was gone. He got up, pushing back the hood on his parka. He started digging through his sled, taking out equipment. Making two piles.

That said it all.

"Six hours?" She pressed him, hating the one-sided conversation more than ever. "Six days?"

Tatum didn't know if she could survive out here on her own. What if another storm blew in? She figured she'd crawl inside the sled with Bandit and the puppies. Wait it out.

We have food now, she reminded herself. *It doesn't take a lot of brains to boil a chunk of meat.* But she deserved to know how long she might be stuck out here.

"Anvil is on the coast, like Wager." Cole finally broke his silence. "You'll smell salt air before you see any buildings. It's probably thirty miles, maybe forty."

Tatum knew the drill. On a good surface that would take three or four hours. Coming back for her on a snowmobile would take another two hours, depending on the weather and snow conditions. She watched as Cole wielded the ax, hacking a caribou shoulder into hunks the size of pot roasts.

"They'll thaw fairly fast in hot water," he said, not looking at her. "Cook them longer for yourself."

Then he tilted her sled, careful of the living cargo, and glazed the runners with ice. "Remember, a glassy surface works best in this kind of snow."

Tatum wobbled from shock as his words sank in. Cole was staying behind—she was the one going for help. Her watch showed 11:20 a.m.

She stared at the dogs, barely getting the words out. "But . . ." Her voice quivered. "Why me?"

"Alyeska, Wrangell, Denali, Kenai. They know the way." He said it simply. "If another storm blows in it's better if I'm the one stuck in one place."

Tatum didn't bother telling him how afraid she was. What was the point? She smoothed her snarled hair into a ponytail and dug out her scrunchie. "You should keep one of the healthy dogs," she said. "Just in case."

"Okay, Kenai can stay with me." Cole took off his gloves. "Take these. They're warmer than yours."

"But—?"

"I have another pair. Chugach, Brooks, Kenai, and I will be here waiting," he said. "I wish we could finish together."

Then he pulled a fur pouch from his pocket. He untied the strings and took out a tan-colored tooth carved in the shape of a bird. It was longer than the one her mom had bought from the Eskimo woman—about five inches, and a lighter color.

"Is that a whale's tooth?" she asked.

"An old one."

"How can something so strong look so delicate?" she asked.

"Elders believe that swallows carry warnings to protect hunters." Cole held the small totem like it was the sun, moon, stars. "Swallows teach us to think quickly. Here, take it with you. It'll keep you safe."

"It's beautiful." It was the closest she could come to good-bye. She put the small bird in the pocket of her parka. Then she lined out the dogs, tied up her hook, and stepped on the runners. "Let's go," she called.

Tatum glanced back at Cole one last time and waved a final farewell.

Her team hesitated, as if they didn't want to leave him. She'd have to earn their respect all over again, now that Cole wasn't with them. "Hike!" she shouted.

Alyeska and Denali ran like they hated it, constantly

twisting to look over a shoulder. Hating it that she was in charge. Tatum wasn't that thrilled with the situation herself. But if she could deal with it, so could they. "Get up there!"

They kept on, dipping into an icy swale. Tatum glanced back again, but Cole had already vanished.

• • •

Tatum knew they were somewhere on the stretch between Wager and Anvil, probably closer to Anvil, like Cole had said.

Might as well be a million miles, she thought. No roads. No other villages in between. Just a barren white landscape that looked the same in every direction.

She couldn't help measuring time: minutes, hours, days. It felt like they'd been out here longer than three days.

None of that mattered to Cole. He didn't even wear a watch.

The air was biting cold. What else was new? No wonder trees couldn't survive here.

Noon was cold.

Two o'clock was colder.

The frozen whiteness went on and on. Tatum glanced at her thermometer. The needle hovered at five below. She ordered her body to make heat.

To keep from being lonely, she thought about weird things. Like the massive sandbar that had once stretched between Asia and North America. Supposedly the sandbar had flooded, and the people who lived there had taken refuge on a rocky island, Santa Ysabel.

She focused on her dogs, barely conscious of anything else. She knew they ran better, smoother, when she let them find their own pace. She didn't think about her mom and dad as much now, didn't listen for the sound of a snowmobile. Being alert and in the present, that was what mattered most.

Two hours on this kind of snow equaled about fifteen miles. They stopped for a snack and moved on. Bandit and the puppies were snug and warm. Tatum could hear the sound of her sled—that was all.

The dogs know the way, she reminded herself, touching the totem through her parka.

They moved in an easy lope, climbing steadily toward a wide saddle. The sides were piled high with snow. It looked like they'd mushed into a giant tub of whipped cream.

The view to the west was flat and straight to the horizon. There was a sameness about it. Tatum felt more at ease now that the dogs were listening to her. "Good going!" she called to them.

The pinks and purples of sunset painted the frozen land. Suddenly a full, guiding moon looked down on her. With moonlight glinting on the ice, she didn't need her head-lamp.

They kept on.

Her three-dog team settled into a no-nonsense stride.

When Tatum felt sleep creeping over her, she knew it was time to make camp. She stopped, set her snow hook as an anchor, and studied the area. Clouds blew in. The moon disappeared. The night turned colorless, empty.

She switched on her headlamp and checked on Bandit. The new mother was lying on her side, licking her nursing bundles of fluff. Tatum's routine was the same as when she had been with Cole: shovel snow into the cooker, add hunks of meat, take off booties and check feet.

While waiting for the meat to thaw, she talked to the dogs and massaged their shoulders. The cooked meat steamed when it hit the icy air. Gobs of grease floated on the water.

Tatum cut up the roast and tossed it out. She fed Bandit by hand. She forced her own dinner down, hating the strong, gamy taste, like the wild animal it was. She ate and ate, finally forcing herself to quit.

You're eating too fast. Too much.

She remembered hearing the story of an Eskimo woman who had been lost in the snow for a week. All those days close to starvation, and she died after being rescued because she'd eaten too much. Tatum doubted it was possible for dogs to overeat.

She tossed around the idea of building a dogloo. She'd never done it herself, but she'd seen enough of them. How hard could it be? She picked up the shovel and went to work. She took her time, not wanting to sweat. Any kind of moisture would freeze. She shoveled a rounded snow cone, hollow inside, and with an entrance.

Alyeska, Denali, and Wrangell watched, their tails wagging hopefully. But when she tapped down the outside, the whole thing collapsed.

The dogs whined.

Then they pawed the snow, circled a few times, and lay down.

19

Tatum climbed inside the sled for her third uncertain night. The heat from Bandit's body warmed the sleeping bag. In turn, the quilted folds warmed Tatum. She curled against her dog, careful not to disturb the puppies. Gently, she reached around and stroked Bandit's fur. "I wonder how Mom's doing?" she whispered.

Bandit whined and wiggled a few inches closer, resting her chin on Tatum's shoulder. The temperature rose even more. "Sleep tight—don't let the bedbugs bite."

Tatum slept, actually slept hard, a deep, dreamless sleep. She couldn't believe she awoke calmly in the darkness. Unless the moon and stars were out, the landscape was all black or all white. *No, that's not true,* she thought, picturing the northern lights.

Outside the sled, the air burned with cold. No morning sounds. No chirping birds. No rustling leaves. Every second it grew colder. She pulled up her face mask and tightened her hood.

They had camped between two cliffs. The walls rose like guards. The taller one looked like a skyscraper and drew her attention. "I hope Anvil's on the other side," she said to herself.

The dogs stirred when they heard her voice. They stood up and shook off. Alyeska and Denali growled playfully. Wrangell had shredded another bootie. Tatum fired up the cooker, wondering what Cole was doing right now. Probably still asleep.

Caribou stew: breakfast, lunch, dinner. The dogs didn't complain. She forced herself to finish a bowl of broth. Before packing up, she sliced off slivers of meat from a bigger hunk and wrapped them in foil. She put the bundle in her pocket. That way, snacking the dogs would be faster.

With Alyeska in the lead, and fatty meat for breakfast, her team ran like a house afire, their ears flat as airplane wings. Tatum had iced her runners like Cole had shown her. They hummed, the kind of comforting sound her mom made when she kneaded bread dough.

Soon, she told herself.

It was more than an hour before the dogs crested a rise that passed between the sentinels. Tatum had been anxious the whole time, hoping to see smoke billowing from chimneys—or at least a sign of village life. Instead she peered down at a frozen field that stretched wide and endless.

"Whoa!" she called.

Tatum set the hook, rushing forward. As far as she could

see, frost heaves, like an eerie army of mounds marching toward her. One behind the other, all the same size and shape.

Her dad had explained what made them. Waterlogged ground expanded when it froze, and pushed itself upward. "There has to be another way," she murmured.

She put Denali in front. "It's up to you now." Then she walked back, tied up the hook, and took her place on the runners. "Let's go!"

Denali hesitated before lunging forward. Slowly, he picked his way over the first frost heave. Tatum relaxed her knees, trying to ride loose. She worried about hitting a chunk of ice. It wouldn't take much to knock her off the sled. No way she could risk an injury.

She squinted against the glare, which was magnified by the whiteness. "Easy now," she told her dogs.

Suddenly the frost heaves were too high, their sides too steep. Her team plowed around them. Every minute was torture. She wondered if they were going in a huge circle. She stopped, snacked the dogs. Wrangell curled into a ball, ready to rest. Alyeska and Denali did the same.

Tatum slumped inside her parka. *Patience.* She had to stay calm, conserve whatever energy she had left. She checked on Bandit. The dog's muzzle twitched as she slept. The puppies snuggled against her peacefully. Sleep and eat. Then do it all over again. That was their life.

Tatum shivered when a breeze ruffled the fur around her hood. The cold was a type of tightness that worked its way under her skin. She felt the carved tooth through her pocket and thought of Grandfather, remembering the light in his eyes.

The spirits live inside him, he'd said with his gentle smile. *They live inside you too. Remember that and you will always be safe.*

She had to trust her dogs.

Shading her eyes, she called them up. "Time to go."

They rose, sniffed the air.

Alyeska began pacing restlessly.

Suddenly Denali was barking like crazy. "What's up?"

Tatum froze. Wolf had stepped out from behind a mound, his fur standing in a stiff ridge on his back. He growled, teeth bared, a low throaty sound. His ruff was rimmed with ice.

She glanced desperately at her team. They slunk backward, showing that they knew who was boss. Wolf had been following them. Why?

Wolf inched closer, silent and glaring. He arched his shoulders. Needles of fear stabbed her. She stumbled back. Wrong move. Now he was in charge.

Tatum knew what she had to do. She yanked off Cole's glove and waved it above her head. "Get back!"

But he didn't stop coming at her.

"Go away!" She ran at him. "Shoo!"

Wolf stopped, ears pressed forward.

Tatum tightened her grip on the glove. Her fingers burned. "I'm lead dog now!" she screamed, then charged again and slapped his nose.

His eyes widened.

"Get lost!" she shouted, louder. "Scat!"

He turned slowly and ran away.

Tatum just stood there, stunned.

20

Once, when Tatum stopped to switch leaders, she glanced back. Wolf had appeared from nowhere a second time, looking fierce as ever. No way they could outrun him.

He's stalking us.

I should toss him a snack to show him we're not the enemy. But the next time she looked, he was gone.

She fired up the cooker. The dogs needed water with their meal. She watched them play tug-of-war with the gangline. *Wolf knows I have food*, she thought. *Maybe that's all he wants.*

After eating, the dogs lay sprawled in their usual places in front of the sled. Alyeska looked ready to nod off; Denali, bored. Wrangell, as usual, was shredding a bootie. Thankfully, Tatum had extras.

She fed Bandit by hand and checked on the puppies. "One day you'll be great sled dogs, born of a great sled dog," she told them. "It doesn't matter if you're boys or girls—you should all have strong names."

"Ancestor," she said. "Because your brow is wrinkled like an old man's." She named the biggest ball of fluff Whale. Then Coal, who was black as beach tar. She thought and thought about a name for the runt. "Skilak, like the lake, because soon you'll be as big and round as the others."

Tatum smeared beeswax on what was left of her bottom lip. She'd had chapped lips before. But this was different, so much worse. Her tongue kept touching the deep split.

She packed up, whispering to the puppies. Ancestor, Whale, and Coal were asleep. Skilak was nosing his way blindly to a teat. All four were well fed and healthy. She loved their sweet puppy smell.

Tatum studied the hummock in front of them. The sun danced on its steep face, casting an inky shadow over the team. She rubbed her sunburned eyes. They felt like someone had poured salt into them.

If I can climb the hummock, she thought, *maybe I'll be able to see something—a chimney or smoke.*

She soon discovered it was impossible to get a foothold in the ice. She stepped back and studied the situation. The slope was too steep. Too slick. She was about to give up when she remembered the ax. What if she chopped steps as she went? It was worth a try.

The first steps she cut were low in the hard-packed crust. The more steps she chopped, the steeper the slope got, and the slower she went. At least her plan was working. The only sound was the ax breaking up ice.

131

Suddenly the wind kicked in. Tatum teetered, cold seeping into her chest. Her lungs ached. Worst of all, she had a killer headache. Probably dehydration.

For courage, she pictured Libby Riddles crossing Norton Sound in a blinding blizzard.

She lifted her left boot and stamped it into the ice, planted her right boot next to it, desperately sucking in air. The ax grew heavier with every strike. She kept climbing, digging in, chanting. Chop, step, breath; chop, step, breath.

Tatum thought about famous mushers. No matter how much experience they had under their belts, they still slammed into trees, pitched sideways down gullies, broke through ice bridges. Frostbitten fingers, toes, noses, cheeks. But they never gave up.

Her icy breath bit into her sluggish progress. *You only fail if you quit.*

Finally, she pulled herself over the frozen lip and collapsed. The glare was as intense as the cold. She breathed into her cupped hands, giving her burning lungs a rest. Her breath glazed her gloves.

From up there the view was spectacular, wide and white. *I've reached the top of the world*, she thought. *Up here, the spirits of native people seem real.*

Tatum stared east over the field of giant hummocks. She wondered how long it would take to mush around them. Distances in nothingness were impossible to judge.

She chopped a chunk of ice and sucked on it, pressing it against her sore lip, but only long enough to stop the throbbing. She didn't want her skin sticking to the ice. She was in awe of the wind-sculpted shapes below. No wonder some mushers didn't care where they finished in the race.

She chopped off another piece of ice and sat in the snow sucking until it disappeared. Gradually the pounding in her head quieted; her lip went numb. She shivered, sticking a wet glove in her armpit.

From the corner of her eye, she saw her three dogs resting in the snow. Their noses were tucked under paws, their eyes watchful. Bandit stuck her head out of the sled, looking around. Tatum had never seen a sight as beautiful as those dogs, their fur shimmering in the afternoon light.

They're my dogs, she thought. *At least for now.*

Her mind shifted to Wolf. He was everywhere and nowhere. She kept imagining his powerful shape and fierce eyes. No way could she outsmart a wolf. They had excellent vision, smell, hearing. "A wolf can smell a deer more than a mile away," her dad had said.

Tatum pulled herself to her feet, searching for her stairway. Going down would be trickier than climbing up. More dangerous, slicker. She found the first step and eased herself over the lip. She used the toe of her boot to find the next step. Not easy. The ice was more brittle than before.

One step down.

Then another.

Tatum clutched the ax. She was afraid of falling through thin ice into a hidden crevasse. She slammed in the blade, just above her shoulder. It stuck. She gripped the handle for balance, feeling for the next step.

She held on, making a slow circle with her boot. Her legs shook. Nothing. *Where is it?* She squeezed her eyes

133

shut, trying to concentrate. A brain freeze could be the end of her.

She pressed her forehead against the ice. Her breathing was shallow. Fear came and went. She pictured the dogs. Bandit and the puppies needed her most of all. Giving up would be the worst kind of selfish.

She opened her eyes and forced herself to focus. Slowly, she braced herself and felt for the next step. It was deep enough for her whole boot. She struggled to work the ax from its slot; her legs shook, fighting for balance. She willed herself on, resetting the ax each time.

A third of the way down, her mind wandered.

She missed a step.

Slipped.

Suddenly, Tatum was in an unchecked slide.

This is what it's like to die!

And everything dissolved into white.

21

Tatum opened her eyes.

A cloud swirled around her.

She lay flat on her back. Her head was spinning. She blinked as the snowy mist settled, and blinked again at the blinding sun. Sweat trickled down her forehead, freezing and crusting on her face.

Climbing the mound had let her know how truly vulnerable she was. She wiggled her toes, then her fingers. She rolled slowly onto her elbow and scooped up a bite of snow. She was limp, exhausted. And darn lucky to be alive.

She looked up, staring at the ax handle. The blade glistened above her head. *Damn!* No way to chop the frozen chunks of meat. And no way she'd go back for it. The ax would fall, just like she had, during the next thaw. She rolled all the way over and sat up, waiting for her head to clear. Her parka and snow pants had cushioned her fall.

Tatum crawled weakly to her feet and brushed herself off.

• • •

Her three dogs were jumping around in their harnesses. Alyeska barked loudest, demanding, *Where've you been?* Tatum pulled them into a group hug and let them lick her face. "I love you too!"

Then she headed toward the sled, and stopped. The sled hadn't moved, but something dark and bulky lurked on the far side. She watched nervously as the shadow turned into a hulking giant.

"Wolf!" She yanked off her glove. "No!"

He was circling the sled, tense and suspicious. Tatum took one slow, careful step, then another, afraid of spooking him. Suddenly, his great wolf head was inside the canvas basket. Bandit made a low guttural sound.

Tatum screamed inwardly, taking another careful step.

Wolf lifted his head from the sled and snarled a warning. His eyes were dark slits.

"Attack me if you want to," she said, lurching forward. She smacked him across the nose. "But stay away from Bandit and her puppies!"

He backed up, stunned by the blow.

His spine bristled, all needles.

"Scat!" She raised her arms to make herself look taller. That was what her dad had told her to do to scare off a bear. She prayed it would work with a wolf dog. "Get lost!"

Wolf sniffed the air, his ears forward in anger.

Tatum glanced wildly from Wolf to the sled and back. She trembled, unable to see Bandit or the pups.

Wolf must be starving.

Tatum choked on the icy air. She lunged at him again, wishing she had the ax. "Scat!" This time she growled like a deranged animal.

Wolf jumped back, his eyes still narrow. Her heart beat furiously. She growled again. Louder. Meaner. She shouted nonsense, just to make noise.

She waved the glove, brandishing it like a deadly weapon. Wolf backed up, avoiding her eyes. Her throat closed around itself, and she quickly checked the sled.

Bandit looked up, smiling her doggy smile. She acted like nothing was wrong. *One, two, three*—Tatum counted the fur balls—*four!* All safe and asleep.

Tatum looked up, amazed.

Wolf had dropped his tail.

"What is it?" She lowered the glove. "What do you want?"

With just a glance, he told her why he was there. She dared to let herself breathe. It went back to that first day at the grocery store.

It took her a while to figure it out. "You knew Bandit was going to have puppies." She kept her voice low, her eyes soft. "Did you want to protect them from a two-legged *kass'aq* girl?"

That had to be it. Instinct from past generations, all the way back to his wolf roots. "Did you think I'd hurt her? Is that it?"

Wolf stood taller, all black against the snow.

Tatum pulled the bundled snack from her pocket. She dropped to one knee and unwrapped it. "Come on," she coaxed, holding out a sliver of meat. "I know you're hungry."

Wolf took a step closer. His whiskers twitched.

"We need you with us." She tossed him a bite. "We need a strong lead dog."

Wolf didn't waste time sniffing it. He gulped, licked his lips, cocked his head, begging for more.

Tatum gathered her courage and scooted forward, talking to him quietly. "You're as smart as you are strong," she said, tempting him with another bite.

Wolf snatched it from her fingers.

When she reached out to pet him, he turned and trotted off. "You'll be back," she called after him. "I have food!"

He yipped a wild note and disappeared.

Tatum felt the afternoon growing shorter. "Food is more important than light," she told the dogs. "But we need water."

Alyeska jumped on Wrangell, and Denali joined them, yelping and rolling in the snow. Tatum fired up the cooker and heated her knife in the hot water. She worked the blade back and forth through the frozen meat. It took forever before the solid roast was in two chunks. Everything took so much time!

"One for tonight's dinner and one for breakfast." Although, she told herself, they'd be in Anvil long before then. She watered the dogs and drank until she thought she'd burst, licking her split lip. "Once we head out we'll run through the night."

Clouds blew in—wispy in pale blues and greens. The

138

sinking sun looked like it was shining behind a pane of frosted glass. Another kind of light show. The slurry of ice crystals told her another storm was brewing. How long before it reached them? An hour? A day? Before moving to Alaska, she'd never given much thought to the weather. Out here, knowing how to read clouds could mean the difference between life and death.

She grabbed her headlamp with a sudden urgency to get going.

22

Tatum's three-dog team ran in single file, with Alyeska in the lead. He jerked awkwardly over the uneven ground. The snow in the gullies between the frost heaves was choppy from constantly thawing and refreezing. Tatum knew ice sometimes grew faster than weeds, then melted and disappeared. It was slow going no matter how many times she glazed her runners.

We stopped too long, she thought. *I shouldn't have climbed the hummock.* What a waste of time! Dogs were so much smarter than people. *I'd be lost without them!*

The dogs warmed up, their muscles rippled. Alyeska, Denali, Wrangell—all running like champions. Their gait began to hypnotize Tatum. She drifted in and out of drowsiness. She blinked hard, stepped off the sled, and jogged beside it to wake up, always keeping one hand on the handlebar.

The air was freezing her from the inside out. She wondered if she had icicles in her hair, like some mushers she'd seen. She lurched back onto the runners. Her mind wandered with every bend. Could frozen hair be snapped off and shaped? An arctic barbershop.

Her chapped face felt tight, like the skin stretched over the hull of a boat. A hot shower. A warm bed. Homemade bread. Playing with Bandit and her pups on a warm day. It didn't hurt to dream.

Alone, she had conversations in her head. Conversations with her mom and dad, conversations with Beryl and Cole. She hated to think of the worry in her mom's eyes.

Alyeska slowed and looked back, as if he wasn't sure he was going the right way. "Come on, now," she said to encourage him. "You're in charge."

Dogs knew their directions without a map, a compass, or stars. Dogs could *smell* their way home. Tatum could see farther than ever before. Through her goggles, she picked out the tiniest prism of light dancing on the snow.

When Alyeska swung wide around another frost heave, Tatum saw two small boys. They looked so strange in a patchwork of fur.

"Hey!" she hollered, hitting the brake hard.

The boys stared at her a long moment before running off. "Ghost girl!" they shouted. "Ghost girl!"

"Come back! Please! I need help!"

"Ghost—" Their voices faded away.

Tatum let the dogs pick up their pace. She followed the boys' tracks over a rise. Up one slope, down the other. She sucked the bitter air. Her breath clouds froze. "Come back!"

She stumbled off her sled, seeing a square house with a peaked roof. It stood alone in a field of white. Dark smoke curled from the block chimney. A snag of driftwood twisted as high as the roof. Kayaks leaned against a wall. Harpoons glistened. She smelled sea salt.

We're close to the ocean.

That meant Anvil.

Our journey is nearly over.

She wasn't sure how far she'd walked, but when she looked back she couldn't see the dogs. She called out, and they answered. *I have to keep better track of where I am.*

Trembling, she rushed to the door.

I made it.

We made it.

She nearly cried.

Tatum knocked on the splintering wood, shaking and listening. The sound of drums and singing swelled from inside. She listened for a long time, wondering what they were celebrating. She knocked again, waiting anxiously. Then she heard a gunshot.

Too tired to think, she stumbled backward.

Grandfather opened the door.

No!

• • •

Alyeska must have brought the team around when she fell off the sled. He stood over her, whining. Wrangell licked her face. She rolled to her knees and sat up slowly. A hallucination. *I was seeing things.*

"We have to stop," she mumbled, trying to clear her mind.

The sun rested on the horizon, yawned, and sank, turning the sky rosy gray.

Tatum took care of the dogs and crept wearily into the sled. She wondered if Cole had already crawled inside his. His dogs would curl up in the snow, like always.

Just a nap, she told herself in the dry bite of night. She cuddled with Bandit and the puppies, letting their warmth settle over her.

She awoke to Bandit's wet nose on the back of her neck. "Hey, girl." She rolled over clumsily. "How're you doing?"

Bandit licked her nose. "Guess I'd better get up."

She couldn't even remember if she'd fed the dogs. *I am losing it!*

She threw back the canvas flap. Dawn had washed darkness from the sky. A band of sherbet clouds looked like it stretched all the way to Nome. Tatum scolded herself, "Some nap!" Was she really heading into day five of this crazy ordeal?

She hollered to the dogs. At first the lumps didn't budge. "Hey! Lazybones!"

Alyeska stood up first. The line pulled on Wrangell and Denali. They stretched sleepily and shook off. Tatum moved in a groggy haze, slow to shovel snow into the cooker. *Shovel?* She felt like kicking herself. *I could've used it to chop up the meat!*

The dogs gorged themselves, like they were preparing for a marathon. Even Bandit ate more than usual. Tatum packed up, tired and shaky. She stepped on the runners. "All right!"

The dogs drove on, heads down, carving their way

around another maze of hummocks. After a few miles, they left the last mound behind. Tatum glanced back, watching it grow smaller and smaller. "Good riddance."

Then she saw Wolf.

She stopped the team and grabbed the bag of meat.

Wolf's eyes grew wide.

"That's right, fella. Meat."

He padded closer, his tail ruler-straight. Frost glistened on his whiskers. She squatted in the snow and tossed out a fatty hunk. He gulped it down in a flash of teeth. The next bite landed nearer. He inhaled it.

Like reeling in a fish, she made each throw closer and closer until Wolf was within petting range. "I have meat and you have muscle," she said, down on one knee. "We'll make a good team."

Wolf thrust his great head forward. He sniffed her glove. She let him lick the grease. Suddenly he took her gloved hand in his teeth. She froze but didn't pull away. "It's okay, fella."

Wolf arched his neck, lifting his head above hers.

She saw his tail move, unsure if he'd wagged it. "We can be friends," she said softly. She slowly wiggled her hand in his powerful jaw. He didn't let go, but he didn't clamp down either. "Come on, Wolf. Friends?"

Wolf shook his head.

"You want to play, is that it?"

He wagged his tail.

"You're not a big bad wolf," she said, letting herself breathe. "You're just a big old puppy dog!"

Wolf whined and let go of her hand.

This time when she reached out, he let her pet him. But only briefly. "Will you take us the rest of the way?"

Tail wagging, he trotted over to the sled. Bandit peeked out. She greeted him, nibbling his chin. Wolf nibbled back.

Wolf, protector of pups and new stepdad, wrinkled his brow.

"Friends," Tatum said simply. "And our new leader."

23

With Wolf in the lead, her team ran better than ever. Strong and confident. At first Tatum had tried snapping him to the line, but she gave up when he flashed his teeth. Alyeska, Wrangell, and Denali followed him obediently, even though he wasn't tethered. They knew he belonged in front.

Sometimes Tatum wondered if they were on the same route as days before, backpacking to Wager. But after an hour it was obvious that they were trailing the arc of the sun, from east to west. Wolf was taking them home, to Anvil, where he was raised. It had to be closer than going back to Wager, like Cole said.

Wolf had started out slowly, letting the team warm up, and kept moving at the same unfailing pace. They climbed along the ridge of an inland mountain. Below, a whirlwind twisted and turned, picking up snow as it left the ground.

Tatum pulled up her face mask and tightened her hood. She kept her eyes on Wolf, running a hundred feet out in front. If he'd only wanted food, he would have gone home long before now. Wolf had followed them because of Bandit and the puppies. What an oddball family they had become.

Wolf dropped his ancient nose, caught a scent, and lifted his tail. Tatum checked her watch. Two hours had passed since they'd left their last camp. Now they were on a snowfield that fanned as far as she could see. The sled glided smoothly on the hardpack until the sun and wind worked at loosening the surface. Then the wind kicked up, blowing hard as ever.

Their fastest pace, barely a crawl.

Just as suddenly they slipped into a calm area. "Wind in the frozen north is like that," her dad always said. "It can crank up and hit hurricane force in an hour, then quit just as quickly."

Tatum held on as the wind struck again, a rumbling wave that frosted the dogs. They struggled against a crosswind. Then all at once it slammed them from behind, invisible hands lifting them up and pushing them forward. Swirling snow blurred the outline of her sled. The dogs turned white.

Tatum tried to keep her head down. Her face mask was clotted with BB-sized ice balls. She gripped the slick handlebars, as if she could keep the sled from breaking apart. Cold sapped her strength. Five days ago she'd been worried about making it back for the flight to Nome. Now she was worried about making it through the next five minutes.

When the visibility was this bad in a race, mushers had to walk the trail from marker to marker. If they couldn't see the wooden stakes, they'd stop and wait for it to blow over. Tatum was about to drop her brake when the dogs pulled up on their own.

Wolf appeared beside her, a white phantom pacing restlessly. His eyes told her they had to stop again. Who knew she'd be so good at waiting?

"Okay, fella."

Using the shovel, she banked the sled the best she could. Her mind conjured up a silly word problem: Wind + Cold = Dehydration. She nearly laughed; her dad would like it.

The dogs hunched their shoulders against the gusts. "We all need water," Tatum mumbled to herself. She crouched beside the sled and reached inside, glad Bandit and her puppies were safely tucked in.

Tatum talked to Bandit as she searched blindly for bottles of fuel. Every one was empty. No way to heat water or thaw meat. *Why weren't we rationing?*

What could she burn? Meat had fat. Fat burned hot. But how could she light it without fuel, as if it was even possible to light a match in hurricane-force winds? She tried not to panic, but everything bad that had happened in the past five days had gotten worse, a lot worse, before it had gotten better.

Shielding her face, she got up and checked on the dogs. She staggered around until she'd touched all four lumps. Wolf was hardest to find, because he was off by himself. They'd forgotten about food and water, only caring about sleeping the storm away beneath insulated blankets of snow.

Tatum wormed her way into the sled and pulled the flap

over her head. She scooched down, struggling to take off her boots in the cramped space. Her socks were damp with sweat. "It's a good thing we stopped."

Bandit whined and nuzzled her affectionately.

She had to take off her gloves to put on dry socks. Her fingers turned to stone. She couldn't feel her toes and kneaded them until they tingled. She swapped her parka for a heavy sweater. To kill time, she turned on her headlamp and picked ice off her face mask.

Then she scooted lower, listening to the wind batter the sled in secret code. If it had a message for her, she wasn't receiving it. The wind would let up for a second, then come slamming back. She prayed it wouldn't roll them over. Cole would be in his sled, just like this.

She turned off her light, fighting to stay awake. "Wait till Mom and Dad see the puppies," she whispered to Bandit. She smiled inside, imagining the puppies big enough to roughhouse. "Beryl's going to be so surprised."

Tatum nodded off. She dreamed she was slapping her alarm clock. It woke her up. She turned on her light and checked her watch. They'd been holed up for about an hour. She loosened the flap and peeked out.

The wind was still whipping, but not as violently. High overhead, the sky had begun to show through the clouds. Wolf had coaxed the dogs to their feet. Tatum wasn't sure they would run without eating first—but they'd starve if they stayed here.

She tugged on her boots and climbed from the sled. She had to trust Wolf's nose to get them out of this mess. Still loose, he took his place in front. Alyeska, Wrangell, and

Denali glanced back. "Sorry," Tatum said, knowing they wanted meat.

Wolf sniffed the wind, tossing his head. He barked an order. His tail went up and they dug in. The earlier winds had probably been more than seventy miles per hour, like the time she and her dad had gone out in a blizzard. Now the air barely moved. The sun burned bright.

Tatum traded goggles for sunglasses. "Come on, now! It can't be far!" She prayed she was right.

Wolf ran with his head down, his ears forward. They dipped into a swale and threaded their way across a flat gully. The dogs ran and ran in the sun and calm air, over ice and soft snow. They ran without stopping, grateful for good weather.

Long into the afternoon Tatum thought she saw tracks. They seemed to appear from nowhere. Did she dare hope?

Wolf turned and looped back to her.

Tatum dropped the hook and walked forward. She blinked at the ruts in the snow, touching them gingerly. They were wider and deeper than those left by a sled. A snowmobile, she realized.

Tracks.

They had to be real, because the dogs were in a frenzy.

24

The endless hours, endless miles, endless worry—impossible hummocks and half-frozen rivers—none of it had prepared Tatum for the sight of a single oil drum, rusted and lying on its side. A half mile later, she saw another one.

She counted seven drums before she spotted a pile of old tires and a beat-up snowmobile. The sight drove the dogs faster and faster. Wolf set a crazy pace. Tatum let him. She didn't worry about them burning out, not if they were this close to the village.

Wolf's going home, she thought, *and my journey is finally coming to an end.*

Fog billowed from beyond a ridge. She looked again, re-alizing it was more than fog. Black smoke smudged the sky. Beautiful black smoke. Nothing had ever looked so good. Dirty smoke and muddy snow. Civilization!

The dogs gathered every morsel of strength they had left

and forged ahead with such speed the sled seemed to rise off the ground. Tatum hung on, laughing. "We really are flying!"

When they flew over a ridge the snow became even dirtier, more like frozen mud. Her runners caught on the hard clods. She heard herself gasp as a dozen frame houses came into view. The air was so clear they looked close enough to touch. And then, finally—the rest of Anvil. Grocery store. Church. Community center. Welding shop. Much like Wager.

Tatum thought she heard a bell. Of course! Kids going to school. It sounded like music. But the sun was on a downward path. No, it must be a dismissal bell. Yeah, kids getting out of school.

The dogs stopped, tongues hanging out. They stared at the village like they couldn't believe it. She could hardly believe it herself. She stepped off the sled, speechless, and took it all in. She blinked at an elderly man leaving a house.

"Hey!" he called.

Is he talking to me?

"Hey!" she called back. Her voice was hoarse in the burning cold.

She'd been cursing deadly weather—snow, ice, and wind—for five days, accusing them of ganging up on her. Yet she'd made it.

Tatum shook hands with her handlebars, throwing her shoulders into the sled. "One more time!" she called.

Wet snow whooshed up from the runners as Wolf led them through the final stretch into Anvil. He kept glancing over his shoulder, tail curled over his back. *This is my village. I brought you home.*

Within minutes, the man greeted her like an old friend. "Are you alone? That looks like Samuel's dog," he said, staring at Wolf.

His gaze slid from Wolf to Alyeska, Denali, Wrangell, and back to Wolf. "You're that girl, aren't you? What happened to the boy? Samuel's nephew? Cole?"

Tatum stared at him, dumbfounded, trying to get a grip on his questions. They came too fast. She looked past the man to the houses, then down at her mud-splattered boots and at Bandit peeking her head out from inside the sled.

"My name's George," he said, smiling.

"I'm Tatum."

"You don't look so great." He swiveled toward his house and shouted something in Yupik. Within minutes a plump woman in overalls, flannel shirt, and work boots trotted out.

"Hot tea!" she said, swinging a canteen. "Here! Drink this!"

Tatum coughed to clear her throat. "Thank you." She uncapped the lid and sipped. The tea tasted sugary—too sweet—but so good that she drank every drop. Even her toes felt warmer.

"You must come inside," the woman said, brushing Tatum's cheek lightly. "Thaw yourself by the stove."

"But—"

"But nothing," George said, already leading the way. "My wife, Umi, doesn't take no for an answer."

"But . . . ," Tatum tried again, her stomach churning. "Cole's still out there. We have to finish together, even if it's not at the same time."

Tatum realized how ridiculous she sounded.

Wolf mouthed her glove affectionately. She slipped it over his brow, scratching his head. His tail drooped, relaxing.

"Wrangell knows where he is," she said. "See the dog chewing his booties? That's Wrangell, Cole's lead dog."

"I'll get a friend," George said, shuffling off. "Rev up our snowmobiles."

Tatum didn't remember everything that happened during the next hour. But Umi fed and watered all the dogs. Wolf gorged himself, then lifted his head, sniffed the wind, and ran off.

"Wolf!" Tatum called.

He kept going, not once glancing back.

"He will return," Umi said. "Samuel is in Nome on council business."

Tatum stared after him. "Wolf!" She felt like crying.

Umi helped hitch baskets to the back of two snowmobiles. They were the size of a small oxcart with skis instead of wheels. George flashed a warm smile, his round face happy as the sun. "We'll bring them all back," he shouted before taking off.

Wrangell raced out in front.

Tatum watched them go, wondering how long it would take before they returned. She pictured Cole loading the caribou meat into the baskets, covering it with tarps . . . Cole straddling the seat behind George . . . the sled being towed like a barge . . . Wrangell, Chugach, Brooks, and Kenai hitching a ride instead of being hitched.

Umi led Tatum inside. She fixed her a bowl of hot soup before taking her to the village doctor. Tatum sat on the examination table, clutching the basket of puppies. Bandit watched from the corner.

The doctor asked question after question. There was disbelief in his eyes when she told him about the past five days. "Get someone to go to Harold's," he barked at the nurse. "Have him radio Fireweed Lodge."

He handed Tatum a tube of ointment for her split lip. "Keep it lubricated," he said, "and we won't have to stitch it."

No way a needle was touching her lip. "Okay."

"Harold's a ham radio operator," he went on. "Phones don't work too great out here."

"A plane will be able to take off from Wager in the morning," Umi added, rubbing circles on Tatum's shoulder. "It won't be long until you see your mother."

Tatum nodded, swallowing the lump in her throat. It was going to be a long night. She wondered if Cole would be able to race in Kotzebue. Was there enough time to rest up?

Bandit suddenly put her front paws on the table. "Don't worry," Tatum said. "The puppies are okay."

She started to climb down, but the doctor told her to sit still. "We're not quite through here," he said, pressing a stethoscope against her back. "Take a deep breath."

She breathed in slowly, staring at her hands. What a mess! Her nails were ripped below the cuticle, clotted with bits of dried blood. She was startled by the sight of her skinny legs sticking out below the cotton gown. They looked like they'd fought Ursus maritimus and lost. Her shin had a long gash, already forming a scab. She didn't remember hurting it.

25

Back at Umi's, Tatum listened to the safe sounds of the small house. It was so much like Grandfather's, too hot and smoky. It smelled like burned cooking oil. There were small appliances scattered around—pencil sharpener, cup warmer, popcorn popper. Black cords snaked over the braided rug.

Umi made Bandit a bed in an open duffel bag and lined it with towels. Bandit slept with her puppies, curled up by the stove. The runt was already plumper. Soon he'd be as big as his sister and two brothers. Alyeska and Denali slept outside on scattered straw.

Tatum scrubbed her teeth with her finger in the shower, then again after she got out with the toothbrush Umi had given her. Umi had laid out clean clothes too: sweatpants, a heavy T-shirt, and thick socks. It took forever to comb the tangles from her wet hair.

Tatum wiped steam off the mirror, gathering enough nerve to look at herself. Her lip was twice its normal size, puffy like cooked sausage. The wound was raw and deep. She winced, smearing on ointment. The circles under her eyes screamed, *Get some sleep!*

Later, over a plate of spaghetti with canned corn, Tatum told Umi about the cabin, the creek with overflow water, and Cole's decision to split up. She was surprised by the calmness in her voice when she talked about Bandit killing the sick caribou. "She saved our lives."

Umi couldn't pass Bandit's bed without stopping to pet her, making clucking noises at the puppies. Bandit licked her hand, smiling her doggy smile.

Umi fixed Tatum a bed on the couch, but Tatum doubted she'd be able to sleep. Not as long as Cole was out there.

Umi went into the kitchen, avoiding the web of cords with practiced steps.

Tatum sat on the floor by the duffel, staring at the flickering fire without really seeing it. "Mom will be on her way as soon as it's light," she told Bandit.

Then she got up and crawled into bed. She heard the back door slam, followed by chattering in the kitchen and the thud of what sounded like a frying pan. She caught a whiff of bacon. Later, a baby cried. She listened to Umi and another woman soothing it in Yupik.

Tatum slept, stirred, rolled, and nearly fell on the floor. She felt limp, exhausted, as if she'd been running all night with her dogs, instead of sleeping on a couch in a warm house. The coals in the stove cast eerie shadows on the walls. Her watch blinked 11:36 p.m. Worry stabbed at her. Cole should have been back by now.

She sat up even though her body begged, *Go back to*

sleep! She reached for Grandfather's totem, which she'd set on the coffee table earlier. Tatum knew the tiny swallow had helped guide her and her team to safety. *Thank you.*

Bandit looked content in her bed by the stove. "Think I'll check on Alyeska and Denali," Tatum whispered. "It isn't right that we aren't together."

Bandit whined softly.

"I knew you'd agree."

Tatum tugged on her boots and grabbed her parka. Her gloves had dried quickly in the hot room. The front door creaked when she opened it. She hoped it wouldn't wake Umi. The sky was clear, with so many stars they looked like one big blur.

She nearly tripped over the dark lump on the porch. "Wolf?"

He got up and stretched his great body.

"Hey, fella." She reached out to pet him, but he stepped back cautiously. "Come on, it's me, Tatum."

Wolf made a slow circle, sniffing. Then he nosed her pocket.

"A midnight snack, is that it?"

Tatum went back inside and walked quietly to the kitchen. Umi had hacked what was left of the caribou meat into pan-sized steaks. Tatum sliced the thickest one into strips, then wrapped it up.

On her way out, she stopped to snack her dog. "Here you go, girl."

Bandit inhaled it.

Wolf was waiting for her on the porch. "Follow me,"

Tatum said. He trotted down the steps, nipping at the bloody package. "Patience, now."

Alyeska and Denali eyed her from their straw bed. "Hungry?" she asked.

They got up and wiggled their rear ends. "I'm happy to see you too," she said, dividing the meat into thirds.

Wolf ate his share, then took off like she'd known he would. A light snow began to fall, turning the streetlights fuzzy. Tatum talked to Alyeska and Denali, grateful for their company.

Through the snowy night she saw the tiniest point of light. It bobbed and disappeared. A moment later, there were two lights. Snowmobiles? She listened intently, hearing the drone of engines. *Finally!*

Author's Note

I was inspired to write *Ice Island* when I visited St. Lawrence Island, Alaska, after the 1,049-mile Iditarod Sled Dog Race. This remote island lies west of mainland Alaska in the Bering Sea—about 230 miles southwest of Nome. Yet it's less than 40 miles from Russia.

It was mid-March, and freezing cold. I had flown to Nome in part to cheer on Iditarod mushers as they crossed the finish line. At the same time, I was promoting my photo-illustrated book, *Dashing Through the Snow: The Story of the Jr. Iditarod*.

While walking the icy streets of the historic gold-mining town, I fell in love with the rustic buildings and the beauty of the frozen Bering Sea. I was amazed to see locals in pickup trucks spinning doughnuts on the ice.

From Nome I flew to a village on St. Lawrence Island. The island has two villages: Gambell and Savoonga. The Siberian Yupik people received title to most of the island through the Alaska Native Claims Settlement Act in 1971. As a result, they legally carve and sell fossilized ivory found there.

Like Tatum in my story, I was picked up at Gambell Airport by a woman driving an ATV. I stayed in a simple rooming house much like Fireweed Lodge. Bundled up against the cold, I wandered through the village and talked to Native men repairing a walrus-skin boat. I learned that it was called an *angyapik* in the Yupik language.

I was startled by the sight of polar bear hides drying on racks, and amused by children playing with large chunks of ice, stacking them like blocks. I remember thinking, *One of these days I'll use these details in a story.*

Some time passed before I created Tatum and Cole and their faithful sled dogs. But I never stopped reading about St. Lawrence Island and its inhabitants. According to my research, the island was part of a land bridge that connected North America to Asia more than ten thousand years ago. It's the sixth-largest island in the United States—over seventy miles long and almost twenty-five miles wide in places.

In *Ice Island*, St. Lawrence Island is called Santa Ysabel Island, and Gambell is renamed Wager. I made the decision to rename them during an early draft when I realized I had to alter the geography to make the story seem plausible.

Today Gambell looks much as it did when I visited it. Unlike Tatum and Cole in *Ice Island*, I never ventured beyond the bounds of the village. And although the temperatures dipped below freezing, I never suffered frostbite or dehydration. Nor did I fall through ice into bone-chilling water.

Glossary

Alaskan husky: A dog of mixed heritage bred primarily as a working dog.

"All right!": The command a musher uses for "Let's go!"

ungyapik: A Yupik word meaning "skin boat."

booties: Socks that protect sled dogs' feet from snow, ice, and exposed rocks. Polarfleece or a durable Cordura fabric is used most often.

checker: A race official who checks each team in and out of designated checkpoints. Racers' mandatory gear is also checked.

drag brake: A flat metal device with claws on the bottom attached to the back of the sled. The musher steps on the brake to slow or stop the team.

dropped dog: A dog that is tired or injured and thus

"dropped" from the race. A dropped dog travels inside the sled to the next checkpoint, where a veterinarian cares for it. After the race, dropped dogs are flown back to Wasilla in a bush plane.

gangline: The main line that runs through the center of the team and attaches to the sled. Each dog is joined to the gangline by the tugline (snapped to the back of the harness) and neckline (snapped to the collar).

"Gee!": The command for a sled-dog team to turn right.

harness: A device that fits over a sled dog's shoulders and along its back, putting the pulling power in the lines. Race rules require that the neck and breast panel of all harnesses be padded. Six inches of reflector tape must be visible on each harness.

"Haw!": The command for a sled-dog team to turn left.

"Hike!": A command that means "Let's go!"

Iditarod: A ghost town approximately halfway between Anchorage and Nome. In odd-numbered years, the Iditarod race follows the southern route passing through the town.

Iditarod Trail Sled Dog Race: This famous 1,049-mile race was organized in 1973 by mushing enthusiasts who feared that the tradition of dogsledding was dying out. The annual event honors the 1925 serum run from Anchorage to Nome, Alaska. It's also called the Last Great Race on Earth.

Jr. Iditarod Sled Dog Race: This race began in 1978 to permit male and female mushers age fourteen to seventeen to compete in a shorter version of the Last Great Race on Earth. The junior route is approximately 160 miles and takes two days.

kass'aq: A Yupik word meaning "white man."

kuspuk: A traditional long-sleeved overshirt worn by Eskimo men and women. A summer kuspuk is lightweight, typically made of cotton. Winter kuspuks are made of heavier material and may be lined with fur.

lead dog(s): A single dog or pair of dogs that runs in the front position. Lead dogs must be both smart and fast.

mandatory gear: Certain items that, according to race rules, mushers must carry in their sled or on their person to ensure good care and safety for themselves and their dogs.

mukluk: A soft, high-top boot made from leather, reindeer skin, or sealskin, and worn by Eskimos.

"Mush!": This command comes from the French word *marcher*, which means "to walk" or "to march." It's rarely used today.

musher: A person who stands on the back of a sled and drives a team of dogs.

neckline: A short line that connects a dog's collar to the gangline.

nenglu: The Yupik word for "igloo."

qamiiyek: The Yupik word for "sled."

quyana: The Yupik word for "thank you."

quyanaghhalek tagliusi: The Yupik phrase for "welcome, thank you for coming."

Red Lantern Award: A red lantern is awarded to the last musher to finish the 1,049-mile Iditarod Trail Sled Dog Race. The longest time for a Red Lantern Award recipient was thirty-two days, fifteen hours, nine minutes, and one second, recorded by John Schultz in 1973.

rookie: A musher participating in a race for the first time.

runners: Two long bottom pieces on a sled that come into contact with the snow. Mushers stand on the portion of the runners that extends behind the sled basket.

serum run: In 1925 untold numbers of Eskimo children in Nome were exposed to diphtheria, a highly infectious disease. A hospital in Anchorage had the only serum in the territory. The serum was put on a train to a native village called Nenana. From there, twenty mushers and their teams of huskies transported the serum 674 miles in a relay. It took approximately five and a half days. The lifesaving serum arrived frozen but still usable.

Siberian Yupik: Indigenous people who live on St. Lawrence Island in Alaska. They also reside on the coast of the Chukchi Peninsula, in the far northeast portion of Russia.

sled bag: A cloth sack that fits into the sled basket and holds the load.

snow hook: A heavy piece of metal with two U-shaped prongs attached to the snub line. Hooked around a tree or stuck into ice, it's used to anchor the team for a short time.

snub line: A rope attached to the sled to secure it to a stationary object, such as a tree.

swing dog(s): A single dog or pair of dogs hooked directly behind the lead dog(s). They help "swing" the sled around curves.

tugline: A line that joins the back part of the dog's harness to the gangline. It's also called the backline.

ulu: An all-purpose knife with a wide, flat blade. An ulu knife has many uses, including skinning animals, cutting patterns from skins, and shaving blocks of ice to build an igloo. Today, a steel blade is common and handles are typically antler or carved wood.

wheel dog(s): A single dog or pair of dogs directly in front of the sled. These dogs are trained to pull the sled around corners and trees.

"Whoa!": A call for the team to stop. It's often used with pressure on the drag brake.

About the Author

Sherry Shahan is the author of more than thirty books, including the Alaska-based adventures *Frozen Stiff* and *Death Mountain*. Her young adult novel *Purple Daze* was written using journal entries, interconnected free verse, and traditional poems.

When she's not snorkeling with penguins in the Galápagos or riding horseback with a herd of zebras in Africa, she can be found studying ballet or competing in West Coast Swing at a dance convention.

Sherry holds an MFA in writing for children and young adults from Vermont College of Fine Arts. She lives in a laid-back beach town in California. Visit her on the Web at SherryShahan.com.